The Secret

Anna Enquist

THE SECRET

TRANSLATED BY
Jeannette K. Ringold

The Toby Press, *London*

First published in 2000 by
The Toby Press *Ltd, London*
www.tobypress.com

Originally published in Dutch as *Het geheim*
Copyright © Uitgeverij de Arbeiderspers 1997

The right of Anna Enquist to be identified as the author of this work has been
asserted by her in accordance with the Copyright, Designs & Patents Act 1988

Translation copyright © Jeannette K. Ringold 2000

Publication has been made possible with the financial support of the Foundation
for the Production and Translation of Dutch Literature.

ISBN 1 902881 07 9 (C)
ISBN 1 902881 12 5 (PB)

A CIP catalogue record for this title is available from the British Library

Designed by Fresh Produce, London

Typeset in Garamond by
Rowland Phototypesetting Ltd., Bury St Edmunds

Printed and bound in Great Britain by
St Edmundsbury Press Ltd., Bury St Edmunds

Part 1

Chapter one

The grand piano hung in the air and was outlined like a burned chop against the snow-covered mountain tops. A grey blanket had been pushed between the black lacquered wood and the cables clamping the instrument. The yellow crane towered above the house like a stiff, one-armed giant, and slowly began lowering its burden. The piano remained hovering just above the balcony, moving gently back and forth. The cables creaked softly, the electric hoisting engine hummed and the sun burned.

Below, in the shadow of the houses, the undercarriage of the crane filled the full breadth of the sloping street. A wedge was pushed against the rear wheels.

When the piano had stopped swinging, people started talking again, children and dogs ran around, sturdy women set down their baskets with vegetables and craned their necks.

There were three movers. One operated the crane, the other two went into the house, the heavy legs of the grand piano under their arms.

The door of the house stood open. A small wheel scraped against the unpainted oak door. When one of the men came back to get the carriage, the pavement was filled with children.

Then the balcony doors flew open and the second man suddenly stood among blue flowers. He looked out over slate roofs, over rolling meadows, over terraces bordered by grey stone; here and there he saw a skinny cow. At the bottom of the valley he saw the narrow silver ribbon of the river.

"I'm lowering," the crane operator called out.

The man with the carriage came out onto the balcony as well; with arms spread both men stood waiting, they reached up to get hold of the grand piano and slowly let it come down on the carriage.

The crane pulled its arm with the cable and the heavy hook back up, leaving the piano behind as an unwieldy load on the balcony.

From inside someone pushed the balcony door open even wider. White curtains fluttered out in the breeze. The men in their cornflower blue coats leaned over both sides of the instrument and pushed it inside, rocking it over two parallel boards.

Downstairs the children cheered. The doors closed.

Chapter two

The space which had been exactly big enough has become too small. There is no peace anymore, the *lubb-dupp* that pervaded everything is drowned out by an increased hissing. Something has to come to an end. It is lost, lost.

The doctor frees the little head with the tightly shut eyes; carefully he helps first one shoulder, then the other to get out. The rubber apron slaps against his shins as he takes a step back to lift up the child.

"An angry little girl."

Metal crashes on marble, the scissors on the countertop; heel protectors scrape over stone; far away water splashes in a wash basin, not like at first, not like at first. There is stinging light, suddenly there is a separation by cold wind and warm hands, there is no air, no air.

Upside down the child hangs in the air, above the mother's spread legs. The fight between gravity and obstinacy lasts and lasts while the onlookers breathe lightly and look fixedly at the bright red little face. Then the child starts to cry.

The nurse has washed the child and wrapped it in a piece of flannel. She lays it in Emma Wiericke's arms, the head on the left arm of Emma who with her right hand is wiping the sweaty blond hair from her face.

The child hears a very soft familiar sound: *lubb-dupp, lubb-dupp*. The small face relaxes and the eyes open, deep blue-grey pools, thinks Emma. This is my child, my daughter, my daughter.

6

Egbert Wiericke kisses his wife. During the delivery he sat in the hall and looked alternately at the people walking by and at his watch. When the nurse finally came out of the delivery room, he let his watch slide into his waistcoat, stood up, and pulled his jacket straight. Silently, he went in. The doctor was just being helped out of his apron and held out his hand to Egbert.

"Congratulations, Mr Wiericke, congratulations! A healthy daughter, seven pounds, twenty-one inches and breathing started naturally; it couldn't be better."

Egbert looked at the forms on the desk. He read, upside down: *Father: Egbert Wiericke, councillor in Leiden.*

Mother: Emma Wiericke, maiden name Orlebeke, no occupation. Time of birth: 18 April 1933, 9:15 AM.

"You may go to your wife now, she's been washed," said the nurse. He turned around, confused, blinded by the glaring light. In the high bed sat Emma with a black spot against her left breast.

"Her name is Wanda, I saw it immediately. Wanda Wiericke, a beautiful name! Don't you think she's beautiful, Eg, won't you say something?"

Egbert gets up from the awkward stool and bends over the bed. He brings his slim, well cared for hand to the small child's head, as if he wants to caress it. His face with the gold-rimmed glasses is two inches from Emma's mouth. She kisses him.

"How are you, Emma? Are you doing all right? I thought it might be difficult for you, it took so long. What a dark baby, her hair looks black."

"That's down," the nurse who is emptying the water basins shouts over the noise of the water. "It falls out and then the real hair comes in its stead. But it sometimes takes a while; then you'll have a bald child."

Emma and Egbert look. The child frowns, it moves the little hands whose fingers with the wrinkled knuckles and the shell-coloured nails seem too large.

Expand and dissolve where there is no more resistance. The head becomes rounded, there is snapping and cracking with each movement. An intense dissatisfaction deep within, the core. A want that pulls the mouth wide open, a desire that becomes a scream. Fright. Silence. Then again the painful emptiness to be screamed at. Bawling, beating the air with the new hands, so empty, so easy. Strike against that softness and warmth, adjust the mouth around what was made for it, pound and beat, beat, beat until the emptiness fills up with contentment from cradling, sucking and singing.

"She's drinking," Emma says proudly. Egbert wipes his glasses clean with his handkerchief. He kisses his wife on her hair and leaves the room.

Chapter three

Bouw Kraggenburg was tired. That whole warm summer day he'd been in meetings in an office palace with artificial air circulation. His mouth was dry and his nose prickled. When he heard the door zoom closed behind him at six-thirty, he tasted the weak smell of rot that hung over the parking area and turned his face to the sun. Home. He placed the heavy black briefcase on the front seat next to him. He didn't feel like being on the highway and continued driving on the old main road, waiting patiently at numerous traffic lights, looking out over the meadows and the water of the Vliet, through Voorburg and Leidschendam to Voorschoten.

In the garden all the plants had bolted and the lawn was too dry. He opened the doors to the terrace, wormed his feet out of his shoes without loosening the laces and took a bottle of mineral water from the refrigerator. Two fingers of whisky. Ice cubes. The newspaper.

Two weeks alone at home. If he were twenty years younger, he would have filled his evenings with engagements that were difficult to justify, with all the things with which he didn't want to offend Johanna. With too much drink and filled ashtrays in the bedroom. Now that he was past sixty, he sat exhausted on the terrace. Glad that he no longer was a practising doctor, that he wasn't on call, didn't have to be on second call. Long live inspection, rather read three thick reports than step into the car in the middle of the night on the way to someone who was in pain and was waiting for him.

Johanna still worked as hard as ever, like him, on the fringes of medicine. She represented a large psycho-pharmaceutical company. She had gone on a two-week trip to Stockholm and Copenhagen to convince colleagues of the superiority of her new anti-depressants. Johanna was seven years younger than Bouw and had never needed her own pills.

There was no wind. The apple tree gave beneficent shade. Bouw took the first swallow of his whisky. The name of the paper was printed in heavy black letters. Under it was a schematic drawing of two entwined hands with the caption: "The *Leidsche Courant* offers a helping hand." Bouw had to smile at it for the umpteenth time and slowly started to turn the pages. A photo of the Rapenburg canal full of

water lilies. A reptile exhibition in the Hortus. The price
of string beans at the vegetable auction. Art. Music tips.
He folded the paper in half and started to read.

PEAK OF DUTCH PIANISM RECORDED ON CD

The landscape of Dutch piano technique has hardly any
mountains. In every generation there have been one or
two virtuosos who have broken through internationally,
but Holland has never become prominent in this area.
More interesting than such superior individuals has
always been the undercurrent of pianists like Goud, Bier-
mans and Laagland who, to be sure, have seldom become
known beyond the borders but who have fascinated
because of a wilful attitude to their profession. Without
doubt Wanda Wiericke belongs to this group. In contrast
to her colleagues, in the seventies she was internationally
considered as belonging to the absolute top. The somewhat
older music lover surely still has her repertoire for piano
solo, as recorded on LPs by Deutsche Grammophon,
standing in the record cabinet. Wiericke became especially
famous through her interpretation of variations and knew
better than anyone how to follow the main theme in
fragmented compositions like Rachmaninov's Etudes
Tableaux *and, her greatest accomplishment, Chopin's*
Preludes.

Deutsche Grammophon *had a contract with her*
and planned to bring out a first CD with these Preludes
and with Bach's Goldberg Variations. *Unfortunately,*

Wanda Wiericke had to cancel this contract when, in the early eighties, she was forced by illness to withdraw from musical life.

The versions which can now be heard on CD were copied from the old recordings. They let us hear passionate piano playing, fiery yet controlled, and adorned by a perfect technique which is always in the service of the music. Over the coming years, Deutsche Grammophon *will bring out a new CD every six months of remastered recordings by this intriguing artist. Recommended!*

Wanda! Bouw was taken aback. He laid the paper on the table. Do you have to keep up with the fortunes of your ex-spouses? Preferably not. He had never really been able to listen to her music again, couldn't stand it anymore. Wanda. He thought she was in America. What was the name of that smooth operator again, that impresario of hers? He'd call him tomorrow. Since Johanna isn't around.

He stood up and stretched. It was close to eight and still the sky was so piercingly blue that his eyes were suddenly filled with tears.

Chapter four

The stones in the floor of the hallway are smooth and soft, black and white. Only with your tongue can you feel where the white stone borders the black. Bitter. In the morning Stina mops the hallway with soap suds. After that she rubs with a cloth, made of an old blanket, over the tiles until they shine. Stina is on her knees. Wanda lies next to her on the floor.

"Come," says Stina, and then Wanda may sit on her broad back, then Stina is the horse. The sun shines through the coloured glass above the door and makes watery spots on the floor. The light spots move from one stone to the next. They climb up along the black umbrella stand, against the coat hooks; the light colours Wanda's coat and, higher up, Mummy's coats. Papa is wearing his coat; he went to his work this morning.

In the kitchen they drink coffee and milk. Wanda, Mummy and Stina. On the big table lie knives, forks and spoons. It's polishing day. Mummy and Stina rub the forks until they sparkle like a mirror in the sun. Wanda gets a small flannel cloth to polish her own fork and spoon. She leans against Mummy's knee and smells the clean cotton apron, the polish, Mummy's perfume.

The women laugh together. Mummy has to rehearse this afternoon, and Wanda will stay with Stina. They'll go and pick beans in the vegetable garden and together walk past the raspberry bush; maybe there'll be enough for dinner. In the back of the garden are pear and apple trees. On the ground lie small, hard little pears that Wanda collects in her doll's pram.

That's the sunny side of the house.

From the black and white checked hallway a dark staircase leads upstairs. That's where Papa's study is, where it smells of tobacco and papers. Wanda is not allowed to go there. When Stina cleans in there, Wanda has to wait in the hall. She runs back and forth impatiently, now she herself is a horse that prances and gallops.

In the vegetable garden you can lie between the raspberry hedges, a long bed of grass. The raspberries are dark patches against the green leaves; the longer you look, the more numerous and the bigger they are.

Between the two green walls there is a sky with drifting clouds that keep making a different painting. Wanda hears the beans drop into the bucket, *plock-plock*. The sound keeps getting duller as the bucket fills up. Eyes close. Stina's gurgling laugh wakes her.

"Come on, they're both gone. I'm alone with the little one."

A heavy object thumps to the ground. Wanda hears a click like a suitcase lock springing open; then a deep, long sigh.

"I'll make something to drink for us," says Stina, "just go ahead."

Soon I'll get up, thinks Wanda, soon I'll go and see who's there.

A song comes blowing through the garden; Wanda lies as if paralysed between the berry bushes. It's a back-and-forth song, a lullaby, under which a humming tone keeps pushing the music along. It sounds like one of Papa's records, but not really. It's music made by someone, but not on a piano.

Wanda gets up and runs out of the vegetable garden. On the bench that stands against the kitchen wall sits a man wearing a cap. On his knees he has a kind of box that he moves in and out. At one end of the box there is a small upright piano which the man plays with one hand, without looking. At the other side of the sliding box is a double row of buttons.

The man taps the ground with his foot, to the beat of the song. Wanda runs towards the music, but then suddenly slows down, three feet away from the man. Stina comes out of the kitchen door, a pitcher of lemonade in her hand.

"Come and take a look, sweetheart, it's something you'll really like! This is Koos with his accordion."

"Accordion," whispers Wanda. Exactly the right word. She gets closer to Koos so that she can hear the instrument better.

The man looks at her for a minute. He has greyish eyes in a totally brown face. He winks. At the back-and-forth point of the song he always holds back a little; then he lets the melody roll down again.

Stina pours the lemonade. She sits next to Koos on the bench.

Wanda sits down on the ground, facing the accordion.

Before Papa comes home, Wanda eats in the kitchen with Stina. Stina places her fingers on her lips: "Lips sealed, right? Koos is our secret, you mustn't tell anyone."

Wanda puts her fingers in front of her mouth as well and nods. She rocks back and forth and sings the song that she heard in the garden.

In the dining-room stand the straight-backed chairs with soft material on them. Papa's chair has arm rests on which he puts his arms. Wanda has taken a bath and climbs on Mummy's lap. A bowl of raspberries stands on the table. Papa looks at the newspaper. "You shouldn't do it, Emma, in these times. It will be misunderstood."

"But it's about the music, isn't it? It's my profession. The conductor is Dutch!"

"But you're singing in German. You should avoid any misunderstanding."

Emma is silent. She hums a waltz melody into Wanda's hair.

"I do understand what you mean, Egbert. But it was agreed on and set up like this. We're doing the *Fledermaus*, and for next season we'll choose a French operetta, I promise!"

Egbert sighs. He takes the newspaper and sits down under the reading lamp. Emma places the dirty plates and glasses on the serving tray while Wanda walks into the garden room through the opened sliding door. The large black grand piano stands there.

Three heavy legs taper down and end in small wheels that each stand on an ebony plate. When you sit under the piano, you see the stomach which isn't black but wood-coloured: thick ribs on which the shiny varnished base is mounted. Two steel cables go to the gold pedals encased in a black pillar that ends just above the floor.

In front of the piano stands a wide stool on which Wanda climbs so that she can reach the keys. Over the keyboard lies a kind of blanket that she pulls away. Then the mysterious realm of black and white is uncovered: islands of two and three raised black keys in a sea of matte-ivory white. Wanda sits on her knees and searches for the song which she heard that afternoon, the swaying movement of one heavy and two light notes above which the melody danced; she finds what she's looking for, on the left she plays the heavy notes and on the right the light ones and she makes up the song to go with it.

Suddenly Mummy is standing behind her and hums along. Now there is a real song above Wanda's playing; it's not exactly the same as what Koos was singing, but it's like it. Mummy sits down at the piano with Wanda on her lap. With her foot she repeatedly gives a touch on the pedal at the heavy note. The sound flowers, continues to vibrate when the key has come back up and mingles with the light sounds above it. Now she sings at the top of her voice: "*Glücklich ist . . . wer vergist . . . was doch nicht zu ändern ist.*" (Happy is he . . . who forgets . . . what can't be altered.)

18   Mummy's hands now play also and make the harmony richer. Wanda's cheeks have warmed up, and she sings along with Mummy.

"Now Wanda is going to bed."

Papa stands next to the piano. He looks as if he wants to slam the lid shut and pull Mummy away. But he says nothing else.

In bed she taps against the heavy headboard with her left hand; then two taps against the side with her right hand. In this way she creates the base for the song, this way she can continue singing without anyone hearing it, without Papa bothering her. In this way she can continue to think up new forms of the song so that it always goes on, always.

*

It's summer. A car has brought Wanda and Mummy to the white house that lies on a dune, in a place that's called Monster. A large square bite has been taken out of the roof so that the corner room is an outside room where you sit under the sky. That's where they eat in the evening, from plates on their laps. You look out over the sea. The waves roll so fast that they crash down. Then they stretch out over the sand, as far as they can.

Sometimes Papa comes. Then they eat inside at the table with the checked cloth. First they sweep, Mummy with the large broom and Wanda with the small one. They sweep together piles of sand on the red tiles. Most of the time Papa isn't there. Wanda lies in her bed listening to the waves, and Mummy reads on the terrace.

On the beach there is a cane chair, a chair like a little room. You can easily sit in it with two people. Mummy reads there too when Wanda is busy at the water's edge. There are many such chairs on the beach. Theirs has cornflower blue pillows, you can see the blue at both sides of Mummy's dress. From time to time Wanda looks up to see if the chair is still there.

"We're going to get something to drink," says Mummy. With their sandals in their hands they walk through the loose sand to the stairs. On the lower treads there is still a lot of sand; as you get higher, you feel the wood through it. At the top of the stairs they have to put their shoes on. Grains of sand chafe against their skin. Over the boulevard they walk to the café with the terrace. Around the tables stand white chairs with curly iron backs. Wanda looks at the sparrows flying from chair to chair, looking for left-over food.

A glass of orangeade, a pot of tea.

"May I use the telephone?" Mummy asks the waiter.

Right back, she said. The iron curls hurt your neck. A sparrow comes and sits down on the plate with cake, its black feet curling around the edge like wires. The bird picks at the cake and inclines its head as if it's looking at Wanda. Stay seated. Make no noise. Right back.

20   In the white house in the dunes, Mummy stands under the shower. She is singing. In front of the small mirror in the bedroom she puts up her hair. Nice smelling stuff on her cheeks. Lipstick. She bites in her handkerchief where there now is a mouth of two red stripes.

"Here, for you. We'll put some perfume on it."

Wanda inhales deeply through her nose. It's not as usual, there is something, a restlessness.

"Is Papa coming soon?"

"No, he won't come until Saturday. Today is Thursday."

Mummy looks in the mirror. She licks her finger and rubs her eyebrows.

The curtains are dark blue. Under them is a stripe of light. The light brushes over Wanda's bed. Here everything is different from at home, but if you sing a song, everything is normal again. Carefully she hums, first with the sheet over her head, then aloud, through the whole room. The song has no words.

When Wanda wakes up, there is no longer any light under the curtains. Sit upright. Climb over the edge out of the bed.

"Mummy?"

It's dark in the hall. Wanda has to pee but the bathroom light switch is too high, and without light it's scary. No one is in the room. Wanda opens the door to the terrace. Empty. The sea whispers, the waves go very gently now that it's night. In the distance are the lights of the boulevard. She climbs over the low stone wall and stands on the path. The broken shells hurt her feet. Wanda runs so fast that the lights rapidly come closer.

The boulevard has smooth grey stones. The terraces are lit up, all the doors are open. The people walking by speak loudly to each other. Wanda sits down on a step. She puts her head on her knees. From the restaurant behind her comes music. The air is warm.

Suddenly Mummy sits next to her on the step. Wanda places her head against the thin material of her dress. She cries. Big bubbles of snot come out of her nose.

Wanda can no longer hold her pee. A small stream runs between her feet, the liquid bulges between the grains of sand. The pajama pants are wet. Mummy picks Wanda up and carries her home. Her high heels scrape over the shell path. At each step Wanda feels sharp nails prick into her thighs.

Chapter five

The movers had screwed the legs under the grand piano and asked Wanda where the instrument should stand. She pointed to the rug in front of the balcony doors without saying anything.

In the kitchen she made coffee for the men and looked for money for a tip. They hardly drank the coffee; they chatted fast and cheerfully and smoked strong cigarettes. Wanda sat on a kitchen chair and massaged her thumb joints. She looked into the room past the men.

Now that she was living in France, she should really have bought a Pleyel. But she couldn't stand that light sound. Affected, superficial. She actually liked the German instruments: Schirmer, Bechstein, and especially Bösendorfer. Steinway has become too smooth, too hard. But reliable.

If only these guys would leave. Now it looked as if she were a pianist, as if she couldn't wait to sit behind that thing, while they were here. But that's not how it was. She no longer knew what it was like to sit down with a sound in your head, with a plan for guiding arms and fingers. Maybe she still knew it, but she no longer felt it.

Stand up, shake hands, utter set phrases of thanks, walk down the stairs. Downstairs Wanda shook the movers' hands once again before closing the heavy door behind them.

Slowly she walked back up the stairs and closed the door of the room behind her, although no one was in the house. At least a third of the room was taken up by the black instrument. She'd been crazy, crazy to have spent so much money for that thing, that apparatus, that monster. Movers, a crane operator, next week a piano tuner. It was a nightmare. As if she could play with these crippled hands, with her crooked back sit on that stool. Why couldn't she leave things as they were? If she missed the music couldn't she just read a score, if need be put on a record?

She sat down on the bench and stared at the piano. Her wrists and thumbs hurt, she pulled the sleeves of her sweater down and stuck the wrapped-up hands under her armpits.

Formerly when she had a headache, muscle ache, or some other discomfort, it would go away when she played.

No magic cures through the secret power of music,

but certainly a lessening of distress through practice and movement. In twenty minutes she'd get rid of a stiff neck by playing arpeggiated triads in contrary motion. Exercises carried out in solitude, because terrible to listen to. Bouw was the only one who liked listening to it; he was intrigued by the gymnastic, the labour aspect of it. He could hear the sounds grow, he heard the tempo increase like a locomotive that gets up to speed, he said.

It was everyday work. Sit down, feel if the stool had the right height. You know that exactly, to the half millimetre, there is no possible doubt about it. Still, during the course of the years she had changed the height of the stool more than once. Sitting high means more power and a better overview, you can pound on the keys with heavy arms. Too high makes the sound hollow and forced, then you no longer fall but instead you start pushing and hitting. The back has no space. Therefore lower. Advantage: the hands hang on the keyboard, the most beautiful legato sound comes into being by itself because the fingers stick to the ivory. The low-sitting pianist has a perfect awareness of his elbows. In the end they prick him in the stomach and then he turns the stool back up. The seat height is a compromise: low enough to be able to feel the weight of the underarms, high enough to be able to oversee the work space.

Slightly to the back on the buttocks. Genitals in contact with the seat. Heels on the floor, right foot flexed smoothly up to the pedal, preferably without shoes, so that the ball of the foot and the start of the toes touch the metal directly, a turned-over spoon against the sole of your foot. Pull the backbone up from the bottom, not hollow but bolt upright in balance above the pelvis, arms high, high and then let them drop, roll shoulders to loosen them, now the neck is completely free, the head can think, and the hands do what they have to.

Carefully Wanda rolled her wrists back and forth and looked at the swollen joints. Her hands have become disobedient servants; tomorrow she will punish them by immersion in hot, stinking water.

She walked past the grand piano without touching it and opened the doors of the balcony. The village lay still in the deep yellow glow of the evening sun; voices and a vague clatter of dishes could be heard coming from the café, for the rest there was not a sound in the whole valley. With a light plastic watering can she began to water the lavender plants, the thyme and the rosemary. Then she sat down between the fragrant pots, her back turned to the room with the black intruder.

Chapter six

The theatre has two marble staircases that wind upward in a curve and meet again on the landing. Above the landing hangs a lamp with a thousand glass pieces that break the light to all sides.

That's where Wanda goes with her father. Egbert Wiericke buys a programme at the bottom of the stairs. He takes the tickets out of his watch pocket, looks at the gold watch and puts everything back again. "We have good seats, in the first balcony."

With his long legs he flies up the stairs, his eyes fixed on the balcony entrance door. The people who want to look at him to greet him turn their eyes elsewhere and fix their hair or their glasses. Wanda clambers up behind her father as fast as she can. The patent leather shoes pinch her feet. Her dress is dark blue velvet. It has a white collar that Stina ironed yesterday.

She would like to stop and look at all the people, at the chandelier and at the paintings of dressed-up singers on the wall. Before Papa pulls her with him into the concert hall, she sees a tall man enter downstairs, alone. He shakes his coat from his shoulders and heads for the cloakroom. The black curly hair is thinner on the top of his head. He looks up for a moment and catches Wanda's eye. Mr De Leon! They smile at each other.

In the hall the lights are still on. Wanda and her father sit down in their seats, at the front of the balcony. There is a gold rail that you can hold on to.

"Be careful not to drop anything," says Papa.

He reads the programme. There is a photo of Mummy in it – she has a very smooth face and she tilts her head, laughing. All the way in the back there is a smaller photo of Mr De Leon.

"Does he take part also?" asks Wanda.

"He's the coach. He practises ahead of time with the singers. Later the orchestra joins in too, and then he doesn't have to play anymore."

Wanda nods. As long as she can remember, Mr De Leon has come twice a week in the afternoon to practise with Mummy. Then the sliding doors to the dining-room are closed and from behind them come the most beautiful songs that you can imagine.

Most of the time Wanda sits with her ear against the

door. Sometimes the piano stops abruptly, and they talk softly, Mummy and her pianist. At the end of the afternoon there is tea; after that Wanda can be the audience and Mummy and Mr De Leon perform the arias that they practised that afternoon.

"I'm not singing," Mummy says once in a while, "I'm not ready to."

Then Mr De Leon plays by himself while Mummy and Wanda sit listening side by side on the sofa.

"Mozart's Rondo, Max, the beautiful one in A minor, would you play that?"

A slow, sad melody rolls through the room, a song that gets more and more grace notes, wanders off, is lost in deep undercurrents but always returns and quietly continues singing to the end. Wanda sighs and is silent.

The lights in the concert hall go out. In the concert pit the musicians are ready to stand up when the conductor enters. Papa said that the story is too difficult to explain. It's about a hairdresser in Spain. Mummy is a girl who is guarded by an older man. Someone is in love with her, but she loves another. Wanda doesn't care; she listens to the overture and sits on her plush chair without moving. It's almost too bad when the curtain opens, you should close your eyes and hear only the voices without being distracted by the walking and dancing on the stage.

A man with a high voice which penetrates to the farthest corners of the hall stands on a table with a guitar in his hands. It looks like he's playing it, but that isn't so;

down in the orchestra pit the violinists pluck their strings with their fingers. The man sings. Mummy appears at the window, she starts singing in response, the same heart-rending song. Suddenly someone pulls her away from the curtains. She screams.

Papa gives the opera-glasses to Wanda. Everything on the stage is suddenly very close. She turns her head a little and all of a sudden sees Mr De Leon's face, in one of the first rows. His dark eyes sparkle. He keeps looking up at the stage.

Wanda waits for the song to return, but that doesn't happen. Someone is tormented, they stuff him into a chest where he doesn't want to be, the choir comes on, and all of them sing a teasing song for the confused man; they carry him away in the chest even though he doesn't under-stand and doesn't want to, he sits up and tries to protest but cannot get through the loud singing.

Then it's intermission. She sees Mr. De Leon walk quickly to the small door underneath the stage. Papa pulls Wanda's arm: "Come, we're going!"

"It's only intermission!"

"It's bedtime."

Papa pushes through the beautifully dressed people, dragging Wanda behind him. Then they stand in the cold evening air, and the theatre doors fall shut behind them.

*

"No, I don't want any coffee, thank you."

Emma smiles and places an arm over her stomach.

Egbert, holding the coffeepot, bends over her shoulder and kisses her. He smiles too.

"Can I get up from the table?"

Wanda slides off her chair and walks into the dark backroom. She climbs on the piano stool and switches on the lamp. Her own music is on the music stand: études by Duvernoy and Burgmüller, recital pieces by Grieg and Bach's Anna Magdalena Notebook. In front of the pedals stands a small bench on which Wanda puts her feet. Oh, if only her legs were long enough now! Mummy says that it's good to practise without pedals, you have to make all the sound yourself and you learn to play beautiful legato. When she takes the duet-book out of the music cabinet, Wanda moves over and lets Emma sit on the side with the low keys. Then Emma reaches for the pedal with her leg. The sound deepens and Wanda can then safely set down her melody in that sea of chords. But sometimes Emma changes pedals at the wrong moment so that Wanda's notes hang bare in the empty air; sometimes she doesn't change at all, and the chords that should be next to each other run into each other. Wanda would rather do it herself.

Finger exercises by Hanon. Feel each finger, the space between the fingers. Then smoothly pass the thumb under, pass the fingers over, the scale. Every day another one. Today it's B-flat's turn. She knows the secrets of the circle of fifths and skips from C to F, to wherever she wants to be. The minuet. Wanda imagines how the dancers slowly turn around each other, always placing their feet solidly on the floor at the first count of every second bar. At the end of the phrase they bow to each other; you can almost hear it.

"She has such an infallible feeling for time, it's unbelievable. And she isn't even six yet!"

Egbert grunts affirmatively. The piano has fallen silent, from the back room comes the sound of rustling paper. Wanda softly sings the melody of the minuet.

"She has to go to school. She does have to learn to read normally. She sits and plays all day long, it can't continue like this, no matter how gifted she is. You also can't continue giving her lessons next year."

"I'd like to. But I'm afraid that I'm spoiling her. She is such a talent, Eg, you don't know the half of it!"

"Next year you'll have other things to do: you'll be pushing the pram! With our son in it, don't you think?"

Emma laughs. There is silence at the table. Wanda starts to practise the Waltz by Grieg, with the delicate melody that wants to go up but keeps falling back. Last week Mr De Leon played the waltz, and Wanda tries to remember, tries to imitate his movements and to make his sound.

Emma tucks Wanda in and sits down on the edge of the bed. Her stomach bulges out above her legs. Wanda places her hand on it. It feels solid.

"When the baby comes, will we still play?"

Emma looks at her daughter, looks at the sturdy hands with the square finger tips.

"That's what I was discussing with Papa while you were practising. I think that you're old enough to have real lessons; I mean no longer from me."

"From Mr De Leon," Wanda says resolutely.

Hand in hand Emma and Wanda walk along the Singel. On the other side of the water the branches of large willows hang right above the water surface. Ducks swim between them as if they are theatre curtains. They walk across the bridge, into a wide street. Next to a store there is a small archway which they enter. They come into a courtyard where there are plants in large earthenware pots. At the far side of the courtyard is a house front with large windows and a door. Out of it steps Mr De Leon.

"Welcome, welcome! Come in!" he says as he opens his long arms wide. He gives Emma a kiss on both cheeks and strokes Wanda on her head. "Sit down, Emma, give me your coat."

Near the heater stand a small sofa and chairs. A table has been pushed against one of the windows. Wanda sees a jam jar with pencils, books, music paper. Mr De Leon lays Emma's coat over a desk chair. Then he takes Wanda with him to look around the room. The whole back wall is taken up by a bookcase in which lie stacks of music. Wanda has never seen so many music books in one place. They turn around to the other window. There two grand pianos stand next to each other, the lids open, a sea of ivory and ebony. "The one near the window is for you. Go and sit down."

He places two thick books under her feet.

Wanda plays the waltz that she has practised. Mr De Leon sits at the other grand piano and plays along with her. He carries her music so that it becomes more beautiful than it already is anyway. When they are finished, he turns around and looks at Emma for a long time. Wanda thinks that he looks sad. She says nothing.

During the night Wanda wakes up. There is no moon, clouds are hanging with a greyish light under them. The street is still and empty. She stands in front of the window and starts crying. It doesn't stop. She doesn't have enough breath and gasps between her sobs.

Emma comes softly into her room, like a ghost in her white night shirt. She brings Wanda back to her bed.

"What's the matter?" she asks. The tears keep running; it takes a very long time before Wanda calms down.

From now on she gets lessons twice a week. Stina brings her to the archway and then goes to do errands. After an hour she is back in the courtyard and they walk home together. Wanda herself carries her music bag with straps on her back Upright.

Chapter seven

"Keizer & Quint Agency, Marina Delblanc speaking!"

"Kraggenburg here. I'm looking for information about Wanda Wiericke. Can you help me?"

"The pianist! Yes, no. One of her concert announcements is hanging right across from my desk. From 1975. Framed. But I don't believe that she's in our database, not anymore."

"Do you have an address where she can be reached?"

"No. If she isn't in the system then I can't find her. Anyway, we're not supposed to give out addresses, those are our orders."

"Who is the director of the agency these days? I assume that the old management has retired?"

"Mr Keizer has passed away. Mrs Quint is still alive, but she no longer works. I've seen her once, at a New Year's cocktail party. Mr Schelling is the manager."

Fred Schelling! Bookkeeper and harpsichord builder. When Bouw met him he was stuffing daily wage envelopes. Now he's the manager of a world-wide artistic company. He surely knows where Wanda is.

"Mr. Schelling isn't here right now, he's on vacation."

"Then I think there's nothing more to be said."

He cut off the conversation before his irritation became audible. To him the diligent Schelling seemed like someone who would connect his telephone to his vacation address.

"Kraggenburg! It's been a long time! No, you're not inter-rupting at all, what's on your mind?"

Schelling didn't know either, except that Wanda, after her father's death, no it was her mother's – old Mrs Wier-icke, the singer – had become ill; the nature of the illness remained unclear but she could no longer play, she had suddenly cancelled everything, right before a tour in Italy. Then Laagland stepped in, with great success as it happened.

"Where is she now, Schelling, does anyone know?"

"Eventually she bought a house in France, in the Pyrenees. We've never known the address, after all we no longer had dealings with her after she retired. It was in the heart of the mountains, Keizer said, totally away from the world. That's not for me, I prefer being on my boat, like now. Listen, I can request her address for you at Deutsche

Grammophon; they must have been in touch with her in connection with making that CD. I'll do it right away! Gladly!"

Bouw was too heavy. He smoked and drank. He was easily tired, or rather lazy. At times he'd think of something to do, but such a plan was seldom carried out. Now a project seemed to be starting with the search for Wanda's address.

Johanna is gone. The children have their own affairs to attend to, I can come and go as I please. The congress in San Sebastian is in a week, my talk is practically ready, my arrangements have been made. I can cancel my flight and get into the car, now. A detour past Tarascon or Luchon or Ax, and then to the coast. If I don't feel like looking her up, I can look around a bit or sit in a hotel. I can take some work along.

He walked upstairs and put a suitcase on the bed.

He reached Johanna in the boardroom of a Swedish hospital.

"I'm going a week earlier. With the car. Are you having a nice time there?"

"Very pleasant. Excellent orders and plans for research. And good food as well. The people are a bit stiff, but I can't go into that because they're right next to me. You won't drive too long at a stretch, will you? It's an enormous distance, to Spain. Is the house too quiet for you?"

"I feel like going away. Drive around down there."

"Can't you just rent a car?"

"That's not the same. I don't want to be tied down."

"Freedom! You act like you're twenty."

Johanna laughed. Bouw thought that he should go North and pluck her away from these proper medical gentlemen; together they would drive over the endless Swedish mountain ridges. But he wanted something different, he wanted to know how things were with Wanda. He had to clear up or check something from the past, something like that, he had to go and see for himself.

He copied an old record onto a tape. Opus 110 and the Variations in C. For in the car. It was six o'clock before he could leave. The freeway was crowded with rush hour traffic, but the car was just back from a big service overhaul and Bouw felt rested and strangely light-hearted.

South of Brussels he ate a beefsteak with a glass of beer, and towards midnight he took a hotel room near Paris. He fell asleep instantly.

The next day all of France lay before his wheels. Along the freeways stood brown signs with drawings of local points of interest. But Bouw realized that he didn't need to see anything anymore. What was worth looking at? People went walking in Nepal, camping in the Grand Canyon, diving in Tahiti. They all had to see it. He too, he had travelled to South Africa, he had travelled all over America and had been in Indonesia. Beautiful, impressive, interesting. But which landscape had he not forgotten, which vistas could he still say he had been happy to see? The Waal river at Hurwenen, the lakes of Bassiès, the sloping fields at Watou, the green hills of Guipúzcoa. That was all. More than these mountains and these waterways you didn't need. This trip took him along everything that he wanted.

He rolled down the windows on both sides so that warm wind streamed into the car. He pushed the tape into the player and let Beethoven compete with the road noise.

Chapter eight

Wanda is six and she can read, ride a bike and almost swim. Her bicycle is too big, the bike repairman has mounted wooden blocks on the pedals so that she can reach them.

When she stays with Aunt Ida during the summer, she is allowed to ride the small red bicycle that used to belong to Suze. Suze is eight already. She can do everything except play the piano. Behind the house in Montfoort there is a meadow with ditches. After dinner Suze and Wanda go there. They rout frogs with sticks and play swimming pool.

"O.K. you! Tread water to the count of one hundred!"

They are very strict. At night Suze whispers about how it is in school. There was a boy who showed his pecker under the desk and everyone was shocked, but it was a candle stump.

In the attic they play with dressing-up clothes. They have babies with whom they're very strict. Wanda is worn out taking care of her children, they are so unruly and they're not very obedient. Then, exhausted, she goes in a blue silk dress to drink a cup of tea with Suze while the babies scream in their cribs.

Wanda tells her about the baby in Mummy's stomach. Her mother is so fat that she can no longer button her dresses. In the dark of the girls' room, Suze tells her how the baby got in there. Suze knows everything. The man puts his prick inside the woman, says Suze. They have to be completely naked, otherwise it doesn't work.

Actually Wanda is hardly shocked. She thinks of Stina, who was giggling and panting when the accordion player stuck his hands under her apron. "Stop that, please stop," said Stina, "can't you see that the little one is there, what will she think?" But the accordion player saw nothing. He buried his brown face in Stina's neck and let his hand crawl up her thigh, just like on his instrument. Although Stina called out for him to stop, she held him tightly and pushed her stomach against his belly. Laughing.

Together in bed, Mummy had said, and then love each other very much.

Wanda lies in bed with Suze. She loves Suze. Yet no real baby comes, for that the strange thing must happen, that Stina thinks about, and the boy in Suze's class, and Suze herself. Now I know it, thinks Wanda, now I know the grown-ups' secret. And I can ride a bike. I know it but I don't believe it. I can't believe that Mummy and Daddy have done it.

"Shall we play father and mother?" asks Suze. "Then we have to take off our pajamas." Under the blankets she pushes down her pajama pants. Wanda lies still but watches as Suze throws off the covers. The bedspread slides on the floor, Suze pulls it back up, leaning on her knees and her elbows. Her buttocks contrast like white swimming trunks against her tanned back. Between the thighs Wanda sees the white labia sticking up like a closed mouth. A red, irritated line shining with vaseline runs along the edge. Wanda pushes her hands underneath herself.

"You have to show your bottom," says Suze when she lies down again. "Come on, you too!"

"No," says Wanda. I don't want to."

*

The canals are frozen over, and on the Singel people skate all day long. You can just walk over to the city without the detour over the bridge.

"The coal merchant sells ice skates," says Emma. "Wanda should get skates, those small children's skates, to learn on."

Egbert goes to get them. They have long, orange bindings with which Wanda can tie them on over her boots.

She goes to the Singel with Stina. They take along a chair and set it down on the ice just like that. Stina bends down and fastens the skates tightly. Wanda's mittens are tied together on a string that goes through her coat sleeves. She can never lose them.

"You have to wear your hat, otherwise your ears will freeze. And always wear your mittens in case you fall."

Wanda stands up. She grabs onto Stina because it feels wobbly, as if she could fall forward any moment and hit against the ice with her hands.

"Hold on to the chair," says Stina. "You first have to practise a little, you know how to do that."

Wanda looks around her. Under the branches of the willow tree the water is open and ducks are swimming around close together. Stina walks over to give them some stale bread.

"There's a hole. You shouldn't go near it, the ice is too thin," she says when she returns. Stina walks very carefully, she doesn't lift her feet but glides over the ice. She moves slowly. The people who know how to skate go fast, on long skates. They bend their backs and make white scratches in the ice.

I'm never going to fall, thinks Wanda. And never skate into a hole. With your hands you cling to the edge of the ice, and then a skater rides across your fingers, he cuts off your fingers and you don't feel it because of the cold. She balls her hands into fists in the mittens and feels a tickling of fear between her legs. Never fall. At the end of the afternoon she is skating, holding Stina's hand. Emma sits on a high chair in front of the window and watches.

Wanda didn't fall once.

*

Doctor Tromp has come. He has put his bicycle in the front garden and comes inside with his small case. Papa himself takes his coat and hangs it on the black coat rack. He shakes the doctor's hand. Both men are equally tall, Wanda sees, but Doctor Tromp is stockier. He fills the whole hall with his large body and steps up to Wanda who is leaning against the wall near the kitchen door. He is wearing high top shoes of sturdy black leather and his trouser legs are held by silver-coloured clamps so that they won't flap into the bicycle spokes.

He shakes her hand as well. A warm, red hand with clean straight-cut nails.

"Well, big girl," says the doctor. He winks. With a quick move of his head he throws back his grey-black hair. Then he goes upstairs where Mummy is lying in bed. Papa follows him.

Wanda goes to Stina in the kitchen.

"It's going to happen," says Stina. "She has so much pain, your mother, it can't last much longer. The doctor is going to help her. It's got to be a boy, she's so heavy."

Everything is mixed up today. It's dinner time but no one talks about eating. Wanda sits down at the kitchen table and looks at the book that she got from Mr De Leon. *Kleine Preludiën en Fughetten* it's called. By Bach, Johann Sebastian. The first piece looks peculiar, with many chords and grace notes for the right hand. Wanda doesn't understand it until she sees that the left hand is the boss, that's where the melody is.

"How you can figure that out, all these black spots!"

Wanda looks up. "I hear it in my head. Sometimes I don't know it, then I just go and play it."

There is screaming from upstairs. Stina walks to the door. Papa and Doctor Tromp come down the stairs.

"We have to go to the hospital," says the doctor. "Where is your telephone, I'll call at once."

Papa goes back up the stairs. Wanda hears Doctor Tromp talk in the hall.

"An ambulance. Now, right away. I'll call the gynaecologist myself. The OR has to be readied for a Caesarean."

He calls another number; it takes a long time before anyone answers.

"I thought that it was a breech, but it's actually a transverse presentation. Impossible to turn. Yes, it's already started. Second child. I'll see you soon!"

45

The ambulance comes to take Mummy. She walks down the stairs herself. Between contractions, says Stina. Downstairs she has to lie down on a small, narrow bed with wheels under it. Her stomach is wider than the bed.

Wanda goes to say good-bye to her. Mummy's face is red. She cries a little but still smiles at Wanda.

"I'll soon be back. With the baby."

Wanda bites her lips and doesn't know what to say. The men from the ambulance service wheel Mummy outside, into the car. Papa goes along. He's put things in a bag for Mummy.

Stina makes French toast. She is going to stay overnight.

"Well make it nice and cosy for the two of us," she

says. In a soup plate she beats two eggs with a little milk.
In it she soaks stale slices of bread which she then puts into
the frying pan.

"Soon she'll forget all the pain and misery, when she
has the little one in her arms. We're going to eat something
nice now, just put your book away."

She sprinkles the golden bread slices with sugar and
a little cinnamon. Wanda would like to eat. French toast
is her favourite dish, and it's nice of Stina to make it now,
but it seems as if the bites remain stuck in her throat and
don't want to go down.

"You father was pretty nervous," Stina babbles. "Men
don't understand, they stand there helplessly. Yes, the child
will come, and with all their learning they can't change
that."

"What's a Caesarean?" Wanda asks suddenly.

"They cut you open over your whole stomach and
then they take the child out. My sister had it. A scar from
your navel to your crotch. And the pain, afterwards! Sometimes it has to be done, if the child is too big or if it doesn't
lie right. Then it can't be otherwise, then you can push till
you die and it still won't work."

Cut open, thinks Wanda. They cut Mummy open to
get the baby out. It's Papa's fault. He made the baby in
Mummy. He was happy, he wanted it. If he hadn't done
it with Mummy, naked in bed – then this would never
have happened.

"Good," says Stina, "At least you're eating. Drink
your milk, then I'll clear the table and we'll play a game.

You don't have to go to bed yet, it's better that we wait together,"

Never, thinks Wanda, he should *never* have done it. It's his fault.

The baby's name is Frank. He sleeps in Wanda's old cradle, at Mummy's side of the big bed. Mummy is always with him. When she comes downstairs, she holds her stomach with both hands. Since she's come back from the hospital, she hasn't put up her hair. It hangs in strands around her shoulders when she sits in her robe at the kitchen table. Wanda looks at Mummy's stomach.

"Yes, it will take time before I'm back to my old self," Emma sighs. "I'm glad that Stina is here, I can't do anything yet. All I do is lie down. I'm happy when you practice, then I have something to listen to."

Wanda goes upstairs with her. Frank has a large, round head. His arms and legs lie unfolded on the small mattress; when Emma picks him up, they hang down limply.

The baby doesn't grow. He gets folds in his skin and his stomach becomes less and less round.

"He doesn't know how to drink," says Emma. "He simply cannot do it."

She has tight bandages swathed around her stomach and also around her breasts. Frank can't get the milk out, he doesn't suck. When Emma puts him at the breast his mouth hangs open right away and the milk drips on his little shirt.

"It's not right," says Emma in the evening, at the dinner table. "Wanda was very different, you felt her in your arms, and she drank like a young calf. I'm calling Tromp tomorrow, it can't go on like this."

"Nonsense," says Egbert. "He's a healthy boy, nine pounds, there's nothing wrong with him."

But Frank cries. Day and night he cries with a feeble, high noise. The white metal scale with the silver weights indicates that he weighs less and less. The big weight is now on the three instead of on the four.

Stina tries with a small spoon that she has formed into a spout with pliers. She holds Frank upright on her lap and carefully pours the milk into his mouth. He coughs, he chokes, but still gets some down.

"Isn't it possible, though, that something is wrong with him?" says Emma. "It seems as if he doesn't see me. Wanda smiled at five weeks."

"Wanda cried too," says Egbert.

"Yes, she screamed and cried when she was hungry, or when she had a dirty diaper. But when I came into the room, she quieted down, she *heard* it, she knew that it would be all right. Frank always cries, whether he's been changed or not. And he doesn't hear me coming. I can't stand it anymore, Egbert, I'm so worried."

Doctor Tromp comes. He looks serious. He gives Frank a nipple with a very long spout so that the milk lands well back in his mouth.

"You have to keep rubbing his lips so that he starts feeling it. And always place his head at an angle in the cradle, then his airways will remain open when he spits up."

Doctor Tromp says much more. He sits in the study with Emma and Egbert, and they talk for at least an hour. In the kitchen Wanda and Stina wait with the dinner. It smells like braised meat; in the garden the trees are already getting fat buds, and Wanda wants to go to the piano but doesn't dare.

Emma comes to tuck her in. She has cried but her hair is pinned up.

"There really is something wrong with Frank," she says. "Doctor Tromp has finally told us, he had to because I insisted. Frank is a mongol. Actually they had already seen it in the hospital, but no one wanted to tell us. Wait and see, they thought. And I kept thinking that it was my fault!"

"What is a mongol?"

Emma takes her handkerchief and wipes her eyes.

"That's what they call a child who can't learn well. They always remain children, they can't become adult."

"Will he die then?"

"No, he can grow up, but he'll still be a child. He won't be able to read and think like you. Everything that he learns takes a long time. That's why he has such difficulty drinking. That's why he doesn't smile at us."

Mongol, thinks Wanda. Mongol, mongol, mongol. Papa's fault. Because he did it with Mummy, because he was so happy with the baby, that's why he got a mongol. Serves him right. Wanda has to cry too. Mummy hugs her.

They both sob. Serves him right, thinks Wanda, serves him right, his own fault.

*

On a beautiful day in May, when Wanda has just turned seven, war breaks out. Are you allowed to play outside when it's war? Are you allowed to make music? The Germans come with tanks and soldiers to grab Holland and boss us around, that's what her teacher in school says. It is obvious that the Dutch soldiers are going to lose. Rotterdam is burning, from the attic window you can see the black clouds. The weather stays beautiful. Mummy doesn't talk about war, she sits with Frank on her lap and tries to feed him. Very softly she sings him a song, even when he doesn't listen. Wanda thinks of the song that Mummy used to sing: *Glücklich ist . . . wer vergisst* – that's a German song and it is beautiful anyway. Bach was German! And Schumann!

Papa comes home from work at an odd time. His face is even more tense than usual. He calls everyone together in the kitchen, Mummy with Frank on her arm, Stina and Wanda.

"It's over," he says. "We've capitulated. From now on only the laws of the Germans apply." He looks at Wanda. "But everyone has a code of laws inside him. That's what we have to listen to now."

Papa places his hand on Mummy's shoulder and looks at Frank who hangs against her arm, drooling.

"We'll care for Frank at home. We won't let him go to an institution and not to a hospital."

His mouth twitches. Mummy places her hand on his.

Wanda counts the faces of her parents and her brother, pale angles in a triangle: one, two, three, one, two, three, one.

"It's all right, Egbert; together we'll manage to get through it," says Emma.

"In music there is no war, music stands above everything," says Mr De Leon. "Your father doesn't really mean that you're no longer allowed to play Bach. What he said about the laws inside you, that's very wise. Your code of laws certainly doesn't say that these preludes are suddenly wrong now, does it? You like to play them just as much as last month. You feel that inside you and that's why you can just continue playing."

Mr De Leon places his hand on Wanda's hair and strokes it. He explains everything that she wants to know and talks about Germany, about the poverty and about Hitler who promises to fix everything as long as everyone just does what he says. He tells her about speeches, boots and marching music. About how difficult it is not to participate in it, about Hitler's hold on the schools and on the children who will soon become soldiers.

He also tells her that not everyone is allowed to belong to Hitler's Germany. Some people are no good according to Hitler's laws. Gypsies, for example, and Negroes, and

Jews. Also people who are ill, or those who have a disability that makes them unable to do all sorts of things, they also are not allowed to participate in the new Germany. They are not valuable, says Hitler.

"So mongols too."

"Yes. That's why your father feels it's so important to care for your brother at home. If you let him be admitted someplace, you don't know what might happen. Your father is a sensible man."

Wanda is silent. Perhaps a German soldier will come to the front door, wearing big boots. He pulls the bell, and she opens. No one is at home. He asks if there are any mongols in the house, and she will show him Frank's cradle. She has to, otherwise he'll shoot her dead. The soldier will walk away with the baby under his arm. She can't do anything about it.

Jews, Mr De Leon said. But what about him? A distinguished Jewish family, said Mummy when Wanda once said that she thought his name was beautiful. He has no disability at all, he can play the piano more beautifully than anyone.

"And what about you?" Wanda blushes. Mr De Leon puts his finger on his lips and smiles.

"My dear, we'll just continue with the lesson. We're going to play Bach."

*

After dinner Emma leaves. Her goodbye kiss leaves a red smudge on Wanda's cheek. Wanda rubs over it and smells the palm of her hand: nice. Through the window of the front room she watches how Emma closes the gate behind her and walks away on high heels. It's evening but it's still light.

Frank lies on the sofa with a pillow against him so that he can't fall off. He lies on his blanket with a rubber sheet under it. His head lies sideways, his fat eyes are two slanting stripes. His mouth hangs open and he can't stop crying.

Egbert has had him on his lap to feed him, but Frank kept letting the long nipple slide out of his mouth. Now Egbert is reading the paper. He sits in the big chair under the lamp and from time to time he looks at the baby.

Why does he cry so, thinks Wanda. He doesn't know that it's war, he doesn't know that Mummy isn't there. Maybe he's hungry, but it doesn't sound like that. He makes a soft, whimpering sound that starts high and then descends slowly. At the lowest point he breathes with a rattle and then starts anew. It sounds sad. It's the only song he knows.

The grand piano stands behind the sofa. Wanda turns on the piano lamp.

"You shouldn't play now," says Egbert, "Frank won't be able to sleep."

"He's not sleeping," says Wanda. She sits behind the piano with her hands in her lap. Her own code of laws, what does her own code of laws say now? She doesn't want to practise but would like to play. There are three kinds of playing, says Mr De Leon. The most beautiful and thrilling thing is playing a piece, thinks Wanda. When a piece is completely finished, when it's in her head and she can play it without the music, then she has to play it. From the door of the music room she walks to the grand piano, singing the piece inside. She sits down, thinks of how it starts and plays it to the end. If something goes wrong, she is not allowed to do it over, not until the next lesson. In a separate notebook, she notes down all the pieces she can play. Sometimes Mr De Leon just picks one out, to see if she still can do it.

Practising is thrilling also, but it takes so long. You have to remember which finger has to play which note, you have to do difficult parts separately, very slowly, so that you barely hear how the piece really goes. You have to practise the right hand and the left hand separately as well. By heart. You have to learn to know what you're doing.

The most fun is: playing through a piece. A new piece, to hear how it is. Old pieces that are not in the playing notebook. Or, what she likes best, four hands. They play from short, wide books and Mr de Leon operates the pedals. You have to listen carefully to each other, follow each other's tempo and way of playing, create the piece together. They do it at the end of every lesson.

Wanda turns off the lamp again. Without really having decided, she is suddenly playing. The prelude with the left hand walking along quietly, and the right hand which plays around it, then goes up and at the end runs amuck. When she starts, she hears Egbert draw an annoyed breath. She continues to play. Playing a piece means never stopping.

After the final chord it is quiet. Wanda looks at her

father. Then they both get up and walk to the sofa. Frank lies looking quietly, his eyes are open. He doesn't cry.

Smiling, Egbert nods at Wanda. Light-headed she goes back to the piano. I have quieted Frank down, Papa is proud, it's going well, I can do it! The second prelude is a triumphant piece, she plays it slowly and solemnly, with *much* sound.

I want him to listen to me, thinks Wanda. To fold up the paper, close his eyes and listen to me. To think: how beautifully she plays, how clever she is, and how sweet.

Very softly the third prelude starts. The fingers touch the keys fast and light like mouse feet. Wanda sits bent over the keyboard, she crawls into the music. She lets it flare up, intense and fast, and then extinguish, always thinking of the man who sits there under the lamp, the man who has to listen and hear. The man who is reading the newspaper.

Chapter nine

She went upstairs earlier than usual, dragging herself up the stairs to the bedroom even though it wasn't even completely dark yet. The contractor had been surprised at her wish to install a bathroom upstairs in the house.

"Do you really want to sleep upstairs, like the chickens?"

That's what she wanted, to sleep next to a large window without curtains, a view of rows and rows of mountains, reaching all the way to Spain. She opened the window. There were no mosquitoes, there was no wind, there was only soft evening air with smells of hay and lavender. Above the mountains still hung shreds of greyish air shot through with pink stripes.

On the floor below stood a black grand piano.

She slept fitfully and woke up at first light. She stretched, five foot nine, shoe size 38. The first questions every new day: where am I, what am I doing here? By sitting down at the piano for the first technical exercises, the answer to this question was resolved. But now? She was somewhere in the south of France, her joints and her hands ached, she was almost sixty, she had no family, no husband, no children.

She was in her own house where no one bothered her. She had escaped obligations and friction.

Sleeping too long just makes people depressed, Bouw used to say. She raised herself up on her elbows. She looked out over the valley. Eagles were supposed to nest above the most distant mountain range; there was a path along a ridge, when you walked there you could see them sailing on the wind. She wondered how eagles sound: like the cawing of crows or the comic grunting of ravens? They would be silent, she thought, the eagles.

She waited until dawn had passed, that dangerous hour. The time of duels, executions, births. When the light had taken hold solidly she got up.

In front of the kitchen window, Wanda had had a roller-blind mounted. Her house was situated at the highest point of the village, and behind it the hilltop was taken up by the extensive graveyard with the church in the middle. From her kitchen at the back of the house she had an ample view of the tombstones decorated with colourful plastic bouquets and framed photos of the dead.

From time to time the inhabitants of the village came clambering up in a black file, the women with headscarves, the men with hats in their hands. They walked slowly on their sinewy legs behind the coffin. The gates of the grave-yard had been opened wide, the high, clear bell chimed incessantly.

On such occasions it was better to pull the roller blind down.

They lay there well, thought Wanda. A prominent resting place under an indestructible stone in the centre of sun, rain and snowstorm.

When would she herself walk along with the procession? When Françoise from the hotel died, or Gérard from the garage. Would they bring her there too, just a stone's throw away? Or would she let herself be transported to the polders of Zuid-Holland?

Doing dishes. It wasn't much: a single knife, plate, glass. The movers' cups. She made the suds and dangled her hands and wrists in the warm water. Hard to believe, she thought, hard to believe. All her life she had protected her hands against everything. Even in September she'd wear mittens, she always had a pair of kitchen gloves with her, she had never worked in the garden, cleaned or done dishes with bare hands. Now she stuck her hands in soapy water with pleasure. Like a dark squid her fingers swam under the layer of foam. Wanda handled the dishes slowly, wiped them clean and set them to dry. She moved her wrists, up and down, back and forth, rotating.

Start every day with a solid half hour of technique, even if it isn't going well, when the body is still sluggish from too much drink, the head slow from too many thoughts. Every day for almost fifty years a different key of the well-trodden circle of fifths. Major and minor days, in tone, tempo and touch; in the same, in contrary motion; in thirds, sixths, octaves. Two against three, three against four. Long and short arpeggios, detached, in contrary motion, with rhythmic variations, with changing accents. Octave skips, blind and while looking, with forearm and upper arm rotation. A wonder, so much sound with so little effort.

A choice from the twenty-five exercises by Brahms. The wrists lead the hands in the complicated arpeggios, low when they move away from the body, high to the middle, they dance opposite each other in front of the keyboard. Always end with the fingers, the end point of the warmed-up machine. The very first exercise by Hanon in which the hand is played out and the thumb keeps landing one note higher. The very simplest. All the large and small muscles are warmed up, all bones stand at the correct angles in relation to each other, breathing is deep and quiet, the body is one with the instrument.

An addictive training, thought Wanda. The hands became muscular like wild animals, the veins were pushed up by the strong hand muscles and meandered over the back of the hand like a blue river delta. Whoever didn't practise was betrayed by the smoothness of the back of the hands. With one glance the teacher knew how things stood. She smiled inwardly, lifted her hands out of the water and carefully started to dry her fingers.

Chapter ten

Stina has become so thin that her apron strings go twice around her waist. There isn't enough to eat, that's why Egbert feels that she has to go.

"She has parents who can feed her, she is welcome on their farm. We can no longer manage, Emma."

"She's happy here. She loves the children. She's honest through and through. I need her."

"I don't want to take any risk. Do you know whom she might tell that at the Wierickes they have a mentally handicapped child in the house? However well-meant, it's a danger that I don't wish to risk."

"You're too suspicious, Egbert. Stina would never say anything, to anyone."

"Still, it's better that she leave. I'll discuss it with her."

Stina packs her suitcase. Her nose is red from crying. She wipes her eyes dry with a corner of her apron.

The last two years she has slept in the small room that really is Frank's. Frank sleeps with Wanda.

Now Stina will leave for Ommen.

"The farm lies on the river. It's called Stegeren. Almost no one lives there; it's very quiet."

"Do they have animals?" asks Wanda.

"Plenty. Chickens, cows, a pig. You could easily come with me, there's enough food. Eggs and milk every day. You could sleep with me in the upstairs room. Shall I ask your parents? Do you want to come with me?"

Wanda considers it. No longer wake up in the sourish smell of Frank's pee. No longer tiptoe in pitch-dark to her bed for fear that he'll wake up startled and will begin to cry. Never again enter the room unsuspecting and see how he has smeared his bed, the wall and his face full of poo. She blushes.

"Do they have a piano?"

"No. But they do have a pump organ. Mother plays it sometimes. With knobs. You can play that."

"They won't let me. I have to stay with Papa and Mummy."

"Well, there are plenty of children who'd go to the countryside if they got a chance. This winter you'll be sorry, when it gets cold. We have a whole forest at the back door, we always have enough wood for heating."

Wanda is silent. She sits with her hands in her lap on Stina's bed, next to the suitcase.

"I understand," says Stina, "you're not the one who can decide that. And for your mother it's better that you stay. Only it's – it's so quiet there, I'll miss you so much."

Wanda nods so that the tears fall on her hands.

"You may never tell anyone how it is with your brother. And I don't want you to bring children from school to the house, understood?"

Full-length, Egbert stands next to the dining table and looks down at Wanda.

"But Eg," says Emma, "Frank is three years old! A child of three can just be at home, whether he's sick or not, that's no one's business, is it?"

"Exactly! It's no one's business and it should stay like that. Anyone can be a traitor. I don't want you to go out with him and I don't want strange people to come in here and see him. He stays here, and here he must be completely safe. I count on you to co-operate. This is the last time we will discuss this."

63

Now that Stina is gone, Wanda has to come straight home from school to watch Frank when Emma does the shopping.

"Come with me," says Gonnie, "you can surely come with me to have tea. Then I'll show you how much embroidery I've already done.

"No," says Wanda, "another time."

Gonnie is tall and sturdy. She has a square face, framed by blond hair, and when she walks the floor shakes. She is Wanda's best friend. In Gonnie's family there are six children, who are all big and talk at the same time with loud voices. Gonnie wants to become a doctor and work for the Red Cross.

"I'm going to marry the ambulance driver. That way we'll always be together. And you?"

"I'm going to be a pianist," says Wanda.

"Aren't you going to marry?"

"No," says Wanda.

Gonnie's father has a taxi. He is turning forty and Wanda has been invited.

"My mother is making a layered pancake dessert, with syrup in between. From me he's getting the embroidery. It's finished."

Gonnie is mad about cross-stitch. With her big hands she embroiders designs in many different colours of wool on pieces of cloth that her mother has cut from a potato bag. Gonnie has first drawn the designs on graph paper. Two cows in a green meadow, with here and there a yellow cross-stitch, like a buttercup, in between. It looks awful, Wanda thinks. But Gonnie's father is happy, he pulls his daughter halfway on his lap and gives her a kiss. She flings her arms around her father's shoulders and leans against him with her large head, her pale eyes closed.

"My big girl," says Gonnie's father. "I'm so happy I've got you!"

With a bang Gonnie's mother sets the platter with pancakes on the table. Suddenly everyone is quiet.

"Enough cuddling," she says. "Go and sit on your own chair, Gon, you're too big for a lap."

She raises the huge kitchen knife and lets it come down with a dull thud straight across the dessert so that the syrup is pressed out at the sides.

When the dessert is finished, Wanda goes home quickly.

Frank sits in the playpen. He coughs. It rattles in his chest when he breathes and his face is warm.

Doctor Tromp comes and pushes up Frank's little shirt. He places the stethoscope against Frank's back and listens.

"I was afraid of that. Pneumonia. It's all plugged up in there again."

Maybe he'll die, thinks Wanda. Then there'll be a war and my brother will be dead. I'll get a new dress for the funeral and everyone will come to shake my hand. How sad, people will think, such a young girl without a brother. How brave she is.

"Why is Frank always sick?"

"Resistance. Little resistance. He should really have a lot of milk, and vitamins. Vegetables and oranges, bananas. None of that is available. And he's extra vulnerable because his mouth is always open. All the bacteria can just come in."

Wanda looks at her brother. His big tongue bulges out. The groove between his nose and his lips is filled with snot. He sits straight up and he hits his legs with both hands at once.

"I'll see what I still have at home," says Doctor Tromp to Emma. "If you come by in the early evening, I'll hand you the medicines. A liquid, I think, because it's so difficult to get pills into him."

"Frankie, Frankie," whispers Wanda. She sits squatting in front of the playpen and looks through the rails. "Do you want out? Shall we play?"

She tries to lift the child but that doesn't work. Then she steps into the playpen, clasps her arms around his waist and pulls him up, over the rim. With a bang he lands on the floor. He falls with his head against the couch and then slides slowly backwards. Wanda is afraid that he'll start crying; she climbs out of the playpen and crawls to him on her knees. She lets her hair brush over his face.

"Frankie!"

"Bwaah," says Frank. That means: Wanda. She takes the rubber sheet and the blanket from the playpen and puts them down under the piano. The blanket is a little wet, just like Frank's pants. She pulls Frank to the piano; she lies down next to him on her knees and elbows.

"Crawl, Frankie, crawl?"

He lies on his side on the blanket and laughs. "Bwaah! Bwaah!"

Wanda's legs are now so long that she can reach the pedals. That's very convenient because it's difficult to do without

them in the Chopin waltzes and mazurkas that she plays.
Mr De Leon doesn't want to play them for her.

"It's better if you discover yourself how you want it,"
he said, shaking his head. "Who am I to show you how
you should play Chopin? Experiment with it for a week.
And then let me hear it!"

In the beginning Wanda thinks it's strange music.
If you play it neatly, like the Bach inventions, then you
can hardly get the curly melody of the right hand slurred
and the piece loses its strength. You have to start every
measure anew. If she uses her right foot, then everything
suddenly changes. The pedal holds the bass notes so that
the piece goes effortlessly from measure to measure and the
curly melodies murmuring are absorbed in the whole.
Elated, she plays for her teacher. He laughs and grabs her
hands.

"You see! Just let these ears and hands of yours do as
they please. You can trust them."

When Wanda has finished playing, Frank is asleep. She
covers him and goes to the kitchen to wait for Emma.
The front door opens, Emma and Egbert come home at
the same time. They are talking animatedly and come into
the kitchen without taking off their coats. Emma has a
small bottle in her hand with the medicine from Doctor
Tromp. It has a strange, orange colour.

"Vaz Diaz and Meijer, both! Rounded up!" Egbert's
face is pale,

"I'm going to give my notice. If colleagues of mine

are treated in that way, I want nothing to do with the court anymore. I should have left last year when they were dismissed. Without grounds. I've been a coward. Now it's enough. I can't live with it, Emma, I can't!"

Emma sits on the kitchen chair and stares at the bottle on the table.

"Do calm down, Egbert. Think it through carefully. Perhaps you can actually do more if you stay on, there are instances of that. Let's talk more about it tonight."

Wanda sits in a corner next to the kitchen countertop. "Frank is asleep," she says to Emma. "I played for him and he fell asleep under the piano."

"I don't want you to drag him around!" Egbert shouts angrily. "Next you'll drop him and he'll break his neck. A child shouldn't lie under the piano, you should stop that nonsense." Wanda is silent, Emma stares. From the other room Frank starts screaming.

Potatoes every night, sometimes with carrots or beets, once in a while with an egg or a small piece of meat. Often Emma makes it into soup, then it looks like more. Wanda and Gonnie look for young dandelion leaves, you can make salad from them. It tastes bitter, actually it's disgusting. Frank eats pablum. He knows how to swallow well now and he's always hungry. He can't feed himself; he throws everything on the floor.

In the middle of they summer a man stands in front of the door with a big package under his arm. He was sent by Stina. There is a pale, flat cheese in the package, and a piece of smoked bacon, a sausage and fifteen eggs, each rolled in a piece of newspaper. Emma is speechless. She invites the man into the kitchen and pours him a glass of Egbert's carefully saved jenever. Stina is well, says the man. There are never any Germans in Stegeren, and everyone goes his own way. Next month is butchering time, and after that people can hunt again, and whoever doesn't have anything to eat catches rabbits. Stina helps her mother with cheese making and she does much more as well, says the man. Emma doesn't ask more. Wanda has gone upstairs to write a note for Stina.

"Dear Stina, it's war. Papa is always angry and Mummy is always tired. Come back, Stina, come back."

Wanda tears up the paper and writes another letter on a new sheet.

Rattling, Frank breathes in his crib and Wanda tries to fall asleep with secret thoughts. She walks onto the stage in a large hall filled with people, they're even in the balcony. Everyone is there: Gonnie with her parents, Papa and Mummy with Frank between them, Doctor Tromp and Stina. Wanda bows and sits down behind the enormously long grand piano. In her mind she plays everything in the right tempo and with the repeats. People have never heard anything so beautiful. They applaud and cheer and give her flowers. At the very back of the hall a dark man stands leaning against the door. He looks at her. She bows. Showered with bouquets she steps off the stage and walks

to the man. He wraps her in his arms and takes her along.
For good.

*

It's so cold at school that the children are allowed to keep
their coats on. Wanda wears Emma's old gloves when she
writes. She has cut off the fingers so that she can hold the
pen. In December the school is closed since no one can pay
attention any more because of the cold. Wanda doesn't
mind. Now she can play the piano all day long. And help
Emma with Frank.

All Frank can do is hit his thighs with his hands, for
hours on end, until his legs are red all over. Emma puts a
pillow on his lap to protect his thighs. Wanda gives him a
wooden spoon and places a turned over bucket between his
legs. Frank is scared by the noise. He screams.

What he likes to do best is bump. He pushes himself
back to the wall on his bottom. He throws his head back
until it touches the wall and then continues pounding. It
reverberates throughout the house.

"You should really take him outside," say the doctor.
"Air and light, that's good for him. Take him along in the
pram when you go shopping."

Emma sighs and shakes her head.

Laundry is the worst. Emma has cut old tablecloths
into diapers. She washes them in the bath tub, with cold
water and grey soap. The clean and the dirty diapers stink
equally bad.

They've stopped using sheets. Franks sleeps on the

rubber sheet that covers the whole mattress. There is a small towel under his head.

Egbert has built a sturdy high chair for Frank. In it he sits at the table. He bangs with his head against the pillow that has been nailed to the back. He sits across from his father. Wanda and Emma sit across from each other as well, at the other sides of the table. They take turns feeding Frank. Wanda keeps thinking of the three-part fugue that she is studying. She says nothing, she concentrates on the three parts and pays attention to how they are interwoven.

When she wants to open the door to the inner courtyard, Wanda sees that his name plate has been taken away. The screw-holes are in the wall.

The heater roars, and together they sit close to it, with their backs to the two grand pianos. Wanda sighs and smiles at Mr De Leon. Soldiers with boots up to their knees, a mongol who bangs his head to pieces against the wall, a pan with urine-drenched rags on the stove. It exists, but not here.

Mr De Leon has the Haydn piano concerto on his lap, the first real concerto that Wanda is going to study. He shows her how orchestra and soloist alternate, leave each other free, or block each other's way. The soloist, thinks Wanda, that's me. She never says anything, at school they call her the quiet one. She sits in class, but she doesn't belong. She lives with Papa and Mummy, but she's different. She has a brother, but she wishes he weren't there. She is a soloist.

Emma has knitted a cardigan for her from blue wool unravelled from an old sweater. It has extra-long arms, with a slit to stick your thumbs through.

During the lesson they solemnly play the whole Haydn concerto. Mr De Leon gives her two books with yellow covers, one about Haydn and one about Mozart. "For Wanda," he writes in them, "a light in dark years."

Frank has to learn how to stand. Egbert pulls him up and holds on to him. Frank's knees are not strong, they buckle in all directions. He falls. Egbert has bought a large, red ball for Frank. He sits Frank upright with his back against the sofa and rolls the ball towards him. Franks starts to cry. He falls sideways and bangs his head against the floor. Egbert sits down next to him and grabs the ball himself. He takes Frank's hand and carefully places it on the ball. Then he rolls it against the wall, lets it rebound and roll back slowly. He grabs the ball before it touches Frank.

You should take off your shoes, thinks Wanda. You should take off these big shiny black shoes when you sit on the floor because that isn't comfortable. You should get rid of these stupid long legs. You should take that stupid child from your lap. You should smash that lousy ball through the window.

She continues reading in her yellow book. At the light of a candle young Haydn copied music that he thought beautiful, until it made his eyes hurt, and then wrote more.

Wanda is standing in the inner courtyard and doesn't know what she should do. The door to the music room is not locked, she has been inside near the grand pianos, near the work table, near the heater. He wasn't there. There was no note. She wanted to stay and wait and perhaps play the new Debussy piece in which the voices run through each other so strangely, like a dream, and that's its name. She didn't dare to touch the keyboard. It had to stay silent. Now she stands between the lavender and the laurel and clasps the music bag against her.

Behind the wall are the sounds of footsteps, stomping, men's voices, in German.

She has to hide, in the corner behind the door, or back in the room, under the grand piano. Her legs don't do what she thinks, they stand stock-still. Her mouth is dry.

Then it's quiet again. Carefully she opens the door and looks into the street. Three soldiers are disappearing in the distance around the corner. Wanda slips outside and runs home.

Frank sits in the washtub and Emma is washing him. With his hands he splashes the water, everything is drenched. Around the corner is the bucket with soiled diapers, but Wanda doesn't smell it.

"He was gone. He wasn't there. There were soldiers." She trembles, everything goes black before her eyes.

"Were you that frightened, dear? Sit down immediately. I can't let go of Frank, I'll be with you right away."

Emma lifts Frank out of the tub and rolls him in a towel. With the child on her lap she sits down next to Wanda who suddenly cries in shrieks. She is still holding her music bag tightly.

After dinner Wanda goes upstairs. She is still trembling too much to sit down at the piano, and she can't think straight. In the slowly darkening room she looks at her shoes. Emma and Egbert are arguing in the kitchen, it sounds like a fugue with two voices that alternate but keep on humming when the other has the theme. Wanda takes off her shoes, goes to the staircase and sits down there.

"Mortal danger!" says Emma. "You know exactly what has happened to your colleagues. Don't you? Round-ups. They storm into the houses and search everywhere. You know that, don't you?"

"He has a place. That's where he was this afternoon. Nothing happened. You don't even know if these soldiers were inside."

"Nonsense. I think that's so cowardly, the way you let things drift. We have a large house; Stina's room is empty. A piano. One more person at the table makes no difference."

"Frank. We attract attention because we have Frank. Because of *him* I don't want to risk anything."

"You're lying, Egbert, you're lying! There is danger and we have to help, it's as simple as that!"

Silence. Scraping of chair legs over the floor.

"Emma. You can ask me anything, I'll do anything. But not this. I beg you: don't ask me this."

The front door bangs shut and Emma's heels drum over the pavement.

When Wanda comes downstairs, Egbert is slumped with his head on the kitchen table. She remains standing in the doorway and clears her throat.

"Where is Mummy?"

Egbert turns his head around slowly and looks at Wanda with red eyes.

"Gone."

The dirty dishes are still on the table. Wanda takes water from the big pan on the stove and makes suds in the dishpan. She smears a daub of grey-green soap in the suds maker and beats and beats and beats in the water. I pound like Frank, she thinks, I smack my father out of the kitchen. Gone. Gone. Gone. She puts the left-over food in a small pan with a lid. Into the outdoor larder with it. First the glasses into the water. Then the knives and the forks. The plates. Finally the pan. Dry everything one by one. Clean up. Wipe the table. The counter top. Empty the dishpan. She puts the bucket with soiled diapers outside, behind the kitchen door. Egbert has gone to the living-room. There is no light. Wanda goes to bed. She waits for the sound of a key in the door.

The next morning Emma has taken her bicycle from the shed. Her face is tense. When she looks at you, she looks farther than your eyes, thinks Wanda, she looks at something that is far away and that I'm blocking. She doesn't

75

look at Egbert at all. He doesn't look at her either, he's helping Frank with his food. Wanda can't eat. Her throat is blocked and there is a rock in her stomach.

Emma buttons her raincoat and pulls a cap over her hair. With her hand on the handle of the kitchen door she says: "I'm going to Ida. If all goes well, I'll be back tonight."

Now Egbert looks up.

"You won't make it on the bicycle. It will be dark when you come back."

"Then that's how it will be. It's not a vacation. It's urgent."

"How do we manage when you're gone?"

"Figure that out yourself. I'm going."

Wanda sees her mother disappear along the Singel, sitting straight on her ladies' bicycle. Over the seat rack hang the floppy panniers in which Wanda used to stick her legs when she was small, when she sat on the back and clasped her mother's waist.

Egbert wipes off the high chair. He has put Frank in the playpen. It's more like a cage, thinks Wanda, much higher than a regular playpen, fastened to the floor planks with brackets.

Her brother sits in his cage.

She picks up her school bag and pulls on her coat. If he asks I'll do it, she thinks. If he asks now if she'll stay with him to take care of Frank together with him, she'll take her coat off again. It happens so often that children don't come to school, they're sick, they suddenly disappear, something has happened – she can easily stay home a day. If he asks.

With stiff steps she walks to school. It's drizzling a little, but there is no wind. It's far to bike to Montfoort. And back. Will Aunt Ida be at home? Is the bridge across the river broken? Then Mummy will have to go by boat. Maybe they'll take away her bicycle. Maybe she'll never come back. What is it in her family, why is it like that?

Step by step Wanda walks past the willows, looking straight ahead. I know what it is, she thinks, it's because of me. Not Frankie, not the war, not Stina, not Papa. Me. It's my fault.

*

Wanda is playing. Frank is already in bed. Egbert sits in the kitchen, but Wanda plays three-part inventions by Bach. Very slowly, in a steady tempo, studying her fingers with extreme attention. When you play Bach, said Mr De Leon, then you tidy up inside, it becomes clean in your head. You have to play Bach every day, throughout your whole life.

The kitchen door. It's well past eight o'clock and yet someone is there. Emma! Without hat and with wet shoes. She's carrying the panniers over her arm and puts them down on the countertop.

"Canned food. String beans. From Ida."

Egbert helps her with her coat. Sitting on a kitchen

chair, she bends down to loosen her shoes. She is so tired that her head remains lying on her knees. Egbert squats down by her and rubs her feet with a towel.

"How was it? Tell me, Emma?"

"Fine. Everything is fine. I was stopped once, on the way back. It was so far. I'm beat."

Emma wipes the strands of hair from her face and puts her arms on the table between the dried plates and clean platters. Wanda is standing in the doorway. She should have put things away. Forgotten. Shall she put the stack of plates in the cupboard now? She takes a step into the kitchen, sees her mother's face and freezes. With piercing, wild eyes Emma looks at her daughter. Emma's mouth is strangely twisted. Gasping she sucks in the air, as if she wants to start crying, as if she's falling into an abyss. Then she suddenly goes limp and her hands slide off the table. The steel meat platter crashes onto the floor tiles. Metal against stone. The sound hangs in the kitchen for a moment.

Emma sits up straight and looks at Egbert.

"Everything is settled. Ida said it was fine. They have someone else there."

"What did you tell them?"

"I told them what was needed."

Egbert is silent.

"Someone will help him across. I have a time and a password. He has to leave tomorrow afternoon. I'll write a note that Wanda can take in her music books. You do have a lesson again tomorrow?" Wanda nods. At twelve-fifteen she wants to say, but no sound comes out.

Emma gets up and takes paper and an envelope from her desk in the living-room. Wanda looks at Egbert.

"Emma," he says, "go and rest first. That letter can wait till tomorrow. You're exhausted."

"No. I can't rest before I've written everything down. Then I can forget it. He has to burn the letter, Wanda, you have to watch that, when he has read it."

Emma writes with jagged strokes, you can hear the pencil scratch against the tabletop.

He is going away. He is going to Montfoort to live with Aunt Ida. As long as there's war. Wanda lies in bed. She bites on her sheet so she won't have to cry. Actually she should be happy. He is in safety. Happy.

She isn't happy. She doesn't want to be without him. Without lessons, without conversations near the heater. What if the war still lasts a very long time? If he wants to stay in Montfoort forever? Tomorrow a lesson for the last time!

Wildly she shakes her head back and forth on the pillow. She's like Frank, she thinks. There's nothing wrong. Mr De Leon is going to live with Aunt Ida for a little while. If she really wants to, she can also go there. On the bicycle. She'll knock at the backdoor and come in. They'll be happy to see her. Suze will want her to stay. They are friends. Every day she'll play with Mr De Leon. They'll take turns practising. She'll hear how he plays. She'll get lessons whenever she wants. They'll eat string beans and applesauce and roasted chicken. It can be done, she'll just do it. It will take some time, but she'll do it.

The following morning Wanda packs her bag next to the piano. The heavy book with the Beethoven sonatas, the études, the mazurkas, and the Bach inventions.

"This is really not right. Sending a child on the street with such a letter. If they catch her, we've all had it. And at Ida's too. Giving a ten-year-old child such a responsibility! We're plain crazy. I'll take it myself."

"That doesn't seem prudent. You're never there, that can cause suspicion. Wanda is at home in that neighbourhood, she's been going there for years, two or three times a week. No one thinks it's strange to see her there. It's dangerous, I agree, but she doesn't do stupid things, you can trust her with such a task."

"I'd still rather go myself," says Emma.

With her bag open, Wanda comes into the kitchen. Emma gives her the letter in a brown envelope. There is no name on it. Wanda sticks it in Bach, at the three-part invention in F minor, number nine, the saddest and most beautiful one that she knows. Then she snaps the bag shut.

"Hand it to him right away," says Emma. "And if there's something unusual, like last time, then you just calmly walk away again."

She is going to save her teacher. Through her he'll get to safety. She'll save him.

All morning long the bag stands against Wanda's legs under the school desk. During recess she remains inside to do extra writing.

Finally the bell rings. In the hall she places the bag between her feet when she puts on her coat.

"Are you coming with me?" asks Gonnie. "No, of course you're having a lesson! You're never able to!"

Wanda nods and walks across the schoolyard. If only no one holds her back now. If only he's home. If only everything goes well. Things will be all right if no one says anything to her anymore. If she meets no one. If she doesn't let go of the bag.

The way from school to her lesson goes through a long, narrow street with stores. Halfway down it there is a slight bend. At the end, the street leads into the wide road where Mr De Leon lives. Wanda walks on the sidewalk, she watches where she puts her feet and has clasped the bag against her stomach with two arms. It's spring, the air is gentle and Wanda is sweating. She is startled when an army truck suddenly comes towards her. The car drives fast, much too fast for such a narrow street. She follows the bend and catches sight of the end of the street. People are standing there, it looks like an obstruction. There are helmeted soldiers. Wanda runs towards it. She squeezes her way through the people who are standing at the barrier and looks. The road is closed to normal traffic. Dozens of soldiers are walking around with guns, with sticks. They prod a long row of people in the middle of the street. Young and old people, men, women, children. Some have the yellow star on their clothes. They all carry baggage, in suitcases, in shopping bags, in cardboard boxes. Groups of soldiers are on the pavement, ringing all the doorbells. They don't wait until someone opens but instead kick the doors to pieces. Then they storm in, screaming. No house is skipped.

The door to Mr De Leon's inner courtyard stands wide open. A soldier comes out who pulls Mr De Leon along by his arm, into the procession. Behind him is another soldier.

The people along the side of the road are dead silent. Wanda crawls under the barrier and stands in the road. She feels the hairs in her neck stand straight on end. A woman pulls on Wanda's sleeve and she stumbles, falls back into the row of onlookers. Mr De Leon has a small suitcase in his hand. He is wearing a black hat and a long, dark coat, without a star. He turns his head slowly and lets his eyes go over the people. He looks at Wanda, he looks through her, he looks past her as if he doesn't know who she is. With his free hand he lifts his hat from his head. Wanda sees the bald spot in the black hair. Solemnly he lifts the hat from his head and puts it back on. Mr De Leon joins the procession and walks with the others to the end of the street.

Part 2

Chapter eleven

Past Fontainebleau Bouw decided to leave the freeway. On the highway you don't belong to the land, you're
pushed through it like blood through the body, imprisoned
in a system of tubes. Freedom, Johanna had said, and that
was what Bouw wanted. But not too much. He knew the
fragile spots in his thinking and knew that being alone for
too long wasn't good for him. The grey ribbon of the
freeway didn't offer enough contact with houses,
clotheslines and people shopping.

   Despite the annoyance of traffic lights and trucks that
were difficult to pass, he felt a calm relief when he had reached
the road along the river. The bicyclists and pleasure boats
made him think of the Amstel. The grass grew haphazardly
on the banks, and in the distance stood rows of poplars.

He shouldn't want to stay here now, he thought. In that case he could just as well have stayed home and taken a short bicycle ride. He had a plan, he had to go someplace. It seemed as if the land pulled at him. He wanted to get going, but he couldn't really manage to.

Pouilly. So that's where that wine comes from. On the other side of the wide river, Sancerre lay on a small peak, a solitary breast in the landscape. At a gas station Bouw got out and stretched. Between the road and the river bank was a park, the grass under the trees had withered or disappeared, children in dirty sneakers were playing there, and old people sat with their poodles on their laps. The river spread a sewer odour.

While the gas station owner took care of the car, Bouw walked around and shook the sweaty shirt loose from his back. The air was shimmering above the asphalt. He walked around the back of the garage and saw that all sorts of small businesses were established in the vaults under the road. Wood lay stacked, there was a repair shop for mopeds, and in the stone arch that lay half under the garage, the gas station owner kept his supply of wine in two large barrels. Bouw went in; it smelled sour and faintly alcoholic. Crates with empty bottles waiting for wine stood on the floor. Along the back wall he saw cans with motor oil.

"You'd have to be crazy to drive at this hour," said the garage owner. "Just enjoy something to eat in the shade. You can leave the car here, it won't get that busy."

A sign, thought Bouw. Someone in this country who puts himself in your place and says something nice without meddling. I'll do what he says. He would take the advice. He would buy twenty bottles of the man's wine. But taste first.

He saw the pitch-black towers of Clermont-Ferrand only in the distance. Now he became ever more lonely among the extinguished volcanoes which seemed to be covered with a green skin. In this moonscape the wild boy of Aveyron had grown up without ever seeing people. That speaks well for the power and flexibility of the land, but speaks against the people. When the boy fell into their hands, they didn't want to understand anything at all about him; they tried to subject him to the rules by which they themselves did so well, and he died. In the introductions to numerous handbooks about the mentally handicapped he will continue to live on, the small wild child. Every policy-maker in health care has to think about him and take a position on the scale of complete individual freedom to total submission to the rules. Lie down on the floor next to the mentally disabled or sit down across from him at a table that was set and teach him to eat with a knife and fork. Of course that wild child wasn't naturally predisposed to be mentally disabled, thought Bouw, but the important period for learning to walk upright had passed without him seeing a loved person manage that trick, and the time for learning to hear and speak a language had passed. He growled, walked on hands and feet and had razor-sharp white teeth. When winter came, perhaps he remembered the previous winter; when the ice melted he must have been elated. But he will never have thought: I no longer crawl as fast as last year. He had no words to sort the past and the coming years. He didn't get to the age of sixty, not by a long shot. Bouw had. He was past sixty and was approaching Albi.

In Albi he took a hotel in the area of the Sainte Cécile Cathedral. He walked through an oasis of well-ordered bricks, past stores with expensive articles in their display windows. Small groups of American and Japanese tourists were walking from the bishop's palace to the basilica, but it wasn't crowded.

From the bathroom window he could see the river, intersected by two stone bridges. Call Johanna? Sweetheart, I'm in Albi, evening is falling and thank God it's getting cooler, shall I go and get some water or some wine after all? No, he'd bridge this fragile spot himself. He had driven here because it was suitable to visit Cecilia before going to Wanda. Johanna had nothing to do with that.

The basilica was actually much more beautiful on the out-side than on the inside. The excessively worked entrance portico protruded from the sober side wall like an intestinal prolapse and gave the visitor a foretaste of the interior. No exaggeration: inside the colours, styles, materials and the lack of emptiness made your head spin.

In the chaos Bouw looked for Cecilia who was hiding between stone garlands. She carried a small organ and her eyes were closed. She had large, solid hands, and that was the only thing that reminded him of Wanda. He continued to stroll over the black and white floor and looked at Old Testament images. Wretched old prophets with despondent faces, nothing to linger over. You could see those at every board meeting.

But not *this*: between the sandstone columns stood a woman who lifted her red dress with both hands to show the point of a sturdy shoe. It was Judith. Her sleeves and her cap were made of gold. She held her head slightly tilted and her face showed no expression. Yes, perhaps concentration; she had squeezed her eyes to slits and seemed to breathe through her slightly open mouth. She was on her way to Holofernes, to tempt him and to kill him. She looked like a pianist about to go on stage to play a Brahms concerto.

Chapter twelve

Buttermilk porridge with dark syrup, potatoes with bacon, fresh sausage and string beans with white beans. Stina calls it "naked man in the grass". Silently Wanda sits at the table with Stina's parents. First they read from the Bible and then they serve. Wanda eats everything. She says nothing, but no one thinks that's terrible. Stina's parents don't say much either. They think that talking is a bother. It slows things down and it easily causes arguments. It's not even needed because everyone knows what has to be done.

"We're going swimming," says Stina. "You can wear my old swimsuit if you want. Or no swimsuit. No one will see us. Come on."

The sun stands high and glistens on the water. Between the fields a path winds to the bank. As far as you can see there is pasture, with here and there a dark green clump of trees alongside it. On the other side of the river stands a skinny horse. With his yellow teeth he rips bunches of grass out of the ground. You can hear the grass tear.

Wanda walks behind Stina. She steps out of her wooden shoes and out of her dress which is really an apron. Stina undresses completely. The large pale breasts hang down freely when she bends to puts down her clothes. Wanda imitates her. She folds up her undershirt and panties and puts them on the dress.

"Come and sit in the sun for a bit, it's good for you. You've got better by being with us!"

Wanda looks at herself. The blisters and sores on her feet have healed. The skin is still a little tight, that's all. Her arms are no longer sticks. However, you can still see her ribs, but much less than before the summer.

"I'm so glad that I took you with me, you were skin and bone, and with those awful chilblains! You've eaten yourself back to shape with our naked man in the grass!"

Now they themselves lie naked in the grass. A little later they slide into the water. There is a light current but not dangerous. In the bend of the river water lilies grow up from the muddy bottom on long slimy stems. The water is brownish and smells of iron and earth. Wanda lets herself float on her back with her eyes closed. She has no thoughts. She feels the water wash through her hair and the sun is warm on her eyelids. She hears Stina splutter as she breathes.

It's still very early when Stina's father drops her at the station in Ommen. She gets a backpack filled with food to take along. In the train she thinks of how it was, in order not to forget. She thinks of the sheets of heavy material. Of the farmer's large hands. That he said: "Come back soon." Of the cowshed where it smelled so pungently and where you sometimes heard a cow hit the wood hard with a hoof. The kitchen where the farmer's wife threw all the leftovers in a bin for the pigs. Sweet and salt mixed. How the grass smelled. The field with the tall juniper berry bushes like black witches in the twilight. The dark starry sky from her window. The silence.

There is no one to pick her up, but that doesn't matter, she knows the way. With the backpack and her travel bag, Wanda walks to her parents' house via the wide street where Mr De Leon used to live. She looks at the paving stones under her feet.

Emma opens the door. "Are you here already! We thought that you'd be coming tomorrow. How wonderful to see you!"

From Emma's clothes comes a sourish smell and her voice sounds tired. It's very dark in the hall when the front door closes. This is home.

Now the dark months begin. For the first time in her life, Wanda works on her school assignments. Every day she does sums and spelling exercises. Next year she'll go to the gymnasium and for that she has to take an entrance exam.

"You don't have to, to become a pianist," Wanda had said.

"No," said Egbert, "but I want you to get a good education. You have the brains for it. *You* do. Then you just have to do it."

But she also has the ears to go into music, thinks Wanda, shouldn't she do that as well? Or do brains come before ears?

She doesn't care too much anymore. Gonnie is also going to the gymnasium. In the afternoon they get extra lessons together from the teacher so that they will be well prepared. Wanda notices that she likes thinking very hard about the solution of a maths problem, meanwhile remembering all sorts of calculations and also taking care to write everything down in a clear manner. Then her whole head is filled and there is no room left to think about music.

She doesn't dare to play. During the last winter of the war she couldn't, it was too cold, her hands went to pieces and she felt weak. In Stegeren there was no piano. Now life is back to normal, and the grand piano is still waiting for her.

Frank is almost nine. He is so big that Emma can no longer lift him. It's a tremendous undertaking to get him to bed in the evening. When Egbert was away once and Emma did it by herself, Frank grabbed the banister and they both fell down. Wanda flew up from her maths problems and saw her mother and her brother lying on the floor. Emma had sprained her ankle and Frank had a bloody nose.

Immediately Egbert built a sturdy bed in the living-room, with a high fence around it that has a small door. Now Frank is always downstairs.

It looks like a stable here, thinks Wanda. My brother lives in a stable, our living-room is a pigsty, and that's how it smells too. Frank moos like a cow. He makes a mess with his own poo. He rocks back and forth and bangs with his head against the wall of the stable.

"You should do much more with him," says the doctor. "A set programme, eat, go outside, sing songs."

Emma and Doctor Tromp sit at the table. Wanda stands in the hall and looks inside through the open door. Teacups. A piece of paper with a prescription. Emma's bare arms. The doctor places his big hand on Emma's hand and with his thumb rubs the inside of her wrist. Emma looks at him, smiles, and then sets her face again. She nods.

"I know. I'm too tired. I feed him, I change him. My husband brings him to bed. Music used to quiet him down. Now we're all exhausted when he finally falls over from fatigue."

She looks puffy, thinks Wanda. Everything about her has become dull: eyes, hair, skin. Frankie is so noisy, she thinks, because she no longer plays for him. It's her fault, but Papa says nothing about it. Don't you play anymore? He asked. When she said that she was too busy with school, he nodded.

Frank has to take a kind of entrance exam too. With Emma and Egbert he goes to a big country house filled with mongols. Doctor Tromp came to talk about it, and now they're going to get acquainted. Emma sits in the back with Frank, and Wanda waves after them.

To the piano. Open the lid. Sit down. Wanda swallows. Carefully she strokes the ivory that has gotten dirty and presses the keys without making a sound. The freed strings whisper.

All afternoon she plays: scales, triads and finger exercises. Even after five minutes she is intensely happy and drunk with the sound.

When she gets up it's nearly evening. She closes the keyboard and sees her music bag standing under it against the wall. Squatting down, she opens the bag: Beethoven, Chopin, Bach. Using two fingers she opens the inventions and looks till she has found the F minor. The letter is gone.

They get new wallpaper and the painters walk around the house in white work clothes. Everything becomes light. Frank is accepted by the institution, and the cage is dismantled. Emma sleeps eight hours every night; she goes to the hairdresser and has the seamstress make a new dress. In the weeks around Frank's move Egbert was quieter than usual, but now he comes home from court early to confer with the painters. In the evening, the three of them eat at the kitchen table which is covered with an ironed tablecloth. Gonnie comes by to do homework, sometimes she stays for dinner and then she tells funny stories that make everyone laugh. Even Egbert smiles when Gonnie drapes a dishtowel around her large head like a turban and shows how Queen Wilhelmina stood waving militantly on the palace balcony on the Queen's Birthday. Gonnie's father had taken her in the taxi; they had gone to eat little pancakes in a stand with mirrors and had never seen that many people together.

"Go and play outside while it's still light," says Egbert. He takes the dishtowel from Gonnie and goes to help Emma with the dishes.

Wanda plays daily, she does two hours of technical exercises and then stops.

"You should have lessons again," says Emma. "Do play something beautiful again, you're doing nothing but scales. Why don't you pick up where you left off with the old pieces?"

"I'm doing calisthenics," says Wanda. She crosses her arms in front of her chest. The forearms tingle and each finger now has its own protective suit of muscles. Control has been restored, the apparatus obeys.

"Shall I look for a teacher for you?"

Wanda shakes no. One day she'll walk through his street and his nameplate will be there again. Then she'll go inside. Then she'll have lessons again.

Wanda has received all nines for her exams because she looked at the questions coolly and without getting nervous. Gonnie, who knows much more, had sweaty hands and a red face. It resulted in sevens.

"You're getting a watch from us," says Egbert. "Saturday we'll go into the city together to choose a beautiful wristwatch for you."

"I don't want that." Wanda looks at her wrists. Everything that is hung around them is in the way of her freedom.

"Why are you so," starts Egbert, but Emma puts her hand on his arm so that he swallows the rest of his words, grim-faced.

"It's Wanda's exam, she'll get a present which makes her happy. Not everyone likes having the time with them. We'll think of something else."

It's supposed to be like that, thinks Egbert. When you go to high school, you get a watch. Why does Wanda always have to be different, isn't her girlfriend getting a wristwatch too?

Wanda slinks out of the room to play her scales.

The next day Egbert comes home with a long package for Wanda. It contains music books: *Das wohltemperierte Klavier*, published by Breitkopf and Härtel in Wiesbaden, two parts. Tears well up in her eyes. The books lie on her lap, her hands which can only do calisthenics lie on top.

The most beautiful thing they could have chosen, the work that he always talked about, that you continue playing your whole life if you are a pianist.

"Are you happy with it, dear?" asks Emma. Egbert coughs and goes to his study.

In bed Wanda reads her new books. It's an edition which has everything: fingerings, slurs, grace notes written out, technical and theoretical comments in four languages. Mr De Leon wouldn't approve of it because with all those

instructions you don't think enough yourself. Wanda
doesn't want to think, she wants to learn, and that works
superbly with these books. This book is my teacher, she
thinks before falling asleep.

*

Wanda likes the gymnasium. There is no time to be bored,
after every hour you get up and walk to another classroom
to learn another subject from another teacher and with
other books. The history teacher is a young man with tight
blond curls that lie on his head like sculptured waves. During the first year he dashed through the most ancient history
at a stiff tempo. Now, in the next grade, he teaches enthusi-
astically about democracy in Greece and the expeditions of
conquest of the Roman army. Wanda likes to listen to him.

98

"Today you can keep your books closed," the teacher
says on a sunny afternoon. "We're not going to do ancient
history but I'm going to tell you about the war, because
tomorrow we'll celebrate the liberation."

His face is red and his voice trembles slightly. He
doesn't remain standing behind his high table as usual but
sits down on the empty first desk, close to the students.
Above his socks Wanda sees a piece of bare leg, whitish,
with hairs. It's the first week in May and Wanda is fourteen.

"Where is your coat?" asks Emma. "What's the matter?
Don't you feel well?"

Wanda doesn't know how she got home. After the
class she raced out of the school, Gonnie tried to follow

her with her bag but she was already around the corner, across the street. She ran until she had a stitch in her side, until she bent over with pain and couldn't go on. She sat by the ditch, she pressed her eye sockets against her knees and repeated *no* a thousand times.

Emma pushes her down on a chair at the kitchen table. She puts a glass of water down for her.

"You should have told me."

Wanda doesn't look at her mother. She has crossed her arms and speaks through her jaws that are clamped tight in anger.

"You knew it. You knew what the Jews . . . What the Germans did to the Jews . . . What they did in the camps. You should have told me."

Emma sits down next to her daughter and puts an arm around her. But Wanda shrugs her off. She stretches and looks at Emma: "This means he's never coming back! He's been murdered. Dead!"

Emma nods. She has become pale. Together they sit at the table. Neither one gets up and neither one can say anything. After a long time Emma whispers: "I couldn't talk about it. I didn't want to know. I wanted it not to be true. It's our fault. We should have made him go into hiding sooner. One day earlier. One day."

"What happened," asks Wanda. "Do you know, did you go and ask?"

"Yes. Deported to Auschwitz. Killed, they think. There. They didn't say how."

How can she sleep? How can she turn off the light and lie down in bed? As soon as she lies down, rows of people in dark clothes start walking and soldiers start screaming. She is nauseated, there is something in her stomach that wants out and she hangs heaving over the sink. The liberating wave doesn't come, the tears stay away as well. Wanda lets cold water run over her face, in her mouth, through her throat. Perhaps he managed to fall out of the train. Perhaps in the camp he wasn't immediately . . . perhaps he had to work there and escaped through fields of tall corn, to the forest. But the line of people keeps walking, with tense faces. If they don't walk fast enough, soldiers hit them in the back.

She wants to be like Frankie. She wants to bang and bang and hurt her head so much that she won't have to see anything anymore and won't understand anything.

But she is Wanda. Mr De Leon in his black hat has walked away and he will never come back. He was flogged into the train and whipped out of it in Poland, he was pushed forward between hundreds of people to a building where . . . Wanda presses her arms around her head and thinks of the invention in F, she thinks of all the voices, very intently, she thinks of which finger she should use for which note, she may not make a mistake, she must know exactly where the arm leads the fingers and where the wrists have to follow obediently, she has to pay attention so intensely that nothing else exists except this melody.

After history class Wanda hangs around in the classroom. She fiddles with her bag while her teacher wipes the blackboard clean. The air fills with chalk. Wanda coughs.

"Is there something you want to ask?" The teacher turns around to face her. He holds up the blackboard eraser as if he wants to continue with his work.

"Yes," says Wanda. "About last week. Did it happen like that, did it always happen like that? Or were there people who escaped, could they flee? You said nothing about that. I would like to know."

The teaches places the eraser on the table and sighs.

"I let myself be carried away a bit by the circumstances. May the fifth. I let myself go. I shouldn't have told you all these terrible things in that way. The principal has called me to account for it. Were you scared by it?"

"Could anyone escape?" Wanda asks again. She looks past him at the smeared blackboard and waits.

"Some went into hiding, you probably know that. And there were indeed escape routes. People sailed to England in small fishing boats, for lots of money. Or they escaped to France and from there were taken to Switzerland, or across the Pyrenees to Spain. Walking! Even when people were already arrested, a miracle sometimes occurred: I know someone who, when he was being herded to the station in a column, walked straight ahead at a bend of the street, right into a row of spectators. The people closed ranks and the man disappeared. Is there someone you're looking for? Have you lost someone?"

Wanda nods.

"And from the train?" she asks.

"I don't think so. That's practically impossible."

The teacher wants to say much more. He has sat down and looks intently at Wanda.

"Thank you," she says, "till tomorrow."

On a warm July day the bell rings and a woman with a vaguely familiar face stands at the door. She has stiffly permed small curls and wears her raincoat buttoned from top to bottom.

"What can I do for you?" asks Wanda. "Have you come to see my mother?"

Emma is already walking to the open door. "Mrs Kooi," she says, "what brings you here? Do come in."

"No, yes, it's like this," says the woman. With both hands she holds a large bag in front of her stomach. "It's about the gentleman who used to live next door to me, you know, where your daughter came for lessons."

Wanda feels light-headed. Can it be that he has sent this woman something? A letter? A sign of life?

Once the three of them are sitting around the teapot, she can no longer control herself.

"Have you received word from him? Heard something, received something?"

"No, my child, that's why. He is not coming back. So many people are gone. We've saved some things, but that's no longer possible. We are moving. I can't take all that with me. It's music, suitcases filled with books. Awfully heavy."

From the answers to Emma's questions it becomes clear that nothing is left of Mr De Leon's possessions. The house has been plundered and a new family has already been living there for quite a while. He packed the music books in suitcases himself and took them to his neighbour.

"For the miss," says Mrs Kooi, looking sidelong at Wanda.

"He said that if he ever disappeared the miss should have his music. Maybe you can come and get it for we have no space for it anymore."

Two full suitcases. Wanda sits on her knees on the floor next to the grand piano and sniffs the smell of old paper. Emma has helped with emptying shelves in the bookcase. The music can lie there. Wanda makes stacks: études, piano concertos, classical, romantic, impressionist, modern. Separate stacks for Bach, for Beethoven, Schubert, Brahms. One stack fourhanded.

She leafs through each book from beginning to end and looks at every page, as if she might find a message between the fingerings and the dashes, as if her former teacher has sent her a letter in a secret language.

*

In her new bra Wanda stands in front of the bathroom mirror. She folds her arms under her breasts and pushes them up. She turns around and over her naked shoulder she looks at the woman in the mirror. Slowly she lets the

straps glide off her shoulders. She turns to her reflection
with half-closed eyes. The bra slides down and she sees the
dark pink nipples appear. With her thumbs she rubs them
carefully, until they become hard and solid and stand up
at an angle. She swallows. She brushes her thick dark hair.
The dress of blue-grey ribbed silk fits her like a glove; Emma
had it made by the seamstress. Wanda got black shoes to
go with it. With a small heel.

With her knees together because of the tight skirt, she
bicycles to Gonnie who is already waiting with Sjoerd.
Sjoerd is Gonnie's boyfriend. They kiss in the bike shed
when he brings her home after a movie. It's the nicest thing
she knows, says Gonnie. You get all weak in your stomach
and you want nothing else. Wanda understands, she knows
that feeling but she can't imagine Gonnie and her boyfriend
necking.

Peter is nice. He's Gonnie's oldest brother, Wanda
has known him for years.

"He's always been in love with you. Invite him to the
school dance, then we'll go together!"

"All right," Wanda had said. Actually had she wanted
to say no, or not? Why can't she be like Gonnie, why does
she get such an unpleasant feeling inside when Peter looks
at her like a faithful dog, why does she feel so ill at ease
when he hangs around her? Because he is nice. And she
isn't. She acts as if she doesn't notice his arm around her
chair. She pushes away from him when he comes closer.
During the dancing she presses against him; later, on the
street, she kisses him because it's dark and because she feels

the silk dress brush against her stomach. When he comes tomorrow to ask if she wants to go with him to the movies, she'll say no again, and then he'll walk down the street heart-broken. No, she isn't nice. She thinks only of herself. She thinks everything is terrible.

"Don't you have to study for school?" asks Egbert. "You're always playing. Don't forget, it's a demanding education, the gymnasium. Before you know it, you're behind."

Doesn't he even *hear* it, she thinks, doesn't he hear that she's playing from his Bach, the book that he gave her? No, he doesn't hear that. He hears school money down the drain, poor grades and repeating a year. Wanda certainly is careful about that. She pays such close attention in class that she doesn't have to do much at home and can browse through Mr De Leon's books for hours.

105

"I've found a teacher for you," says Emma. "She has just come from America. Her husband works in the orchestra here. A very good pianist. Wednesday at three o'clock. You have to take along something to play, an étude and something by Bach."

Mrs Heidelberg lives on the top floor of a house on a canal. Accompanied by an impatient voice calling out "upstairs, upstairs!" at short intervals, Wanda stumbles through a maze of halls and staircases, open and closed doors.

In a sea of light stands a heavy woman, dressed in draped lengths of cloth. Her right arm leans on a brown grand piano with an open lid. On the back of her hand and even on the back of her fingers there are plump fleshy pillows, like a baby's.

For a moment Wanda is blinded by the sun which falls through the wide windows. She smells cigarette smoke and hears the raw, rasping voice.

"So, you're big. Do you have the curse yet?"

Wanda is startled. What does she mean? What does she know? Instinctively she thinks of Frank; are you cursed if you have such a brother? Or another curse, one that has to do with the war, with disloyalty and negligence? That I let people who cared about me just go away – she can't know that, she should stay out of that!

With two hands Mrs Heidelberg motions in the direction of her lap: "The curse, menstruation!"

Oh! Wanda nods.

Mrs Heidelberg says that she doesn't have time to give lessons, she is a concert pianist, she has to practise.

"But your mother is my friend from long ago. So sit down and play."

Wanda sets down her bag and takes off her coat. There is no place to hang it up, so she just places it on the floor. Painted wood. Under the grand piano lies a rug. She tries the piano stool and turns it down lower. Mrs Heidelberg sniffs and sits down far away in a corner, next to an ashtray on a pillar.

Wanda lets her arms hang loose next to her body and with her feet feels the weight of the pedals. Almost imperceptibly she moves her upper body in the tempo of the étude that she is going to play. In the back of the book with the Chopin études that are much too difficult she found a short one that looked playable. It is a rhythmic exercise, the melody has triplets against four eighth notes in the accompaniment; it is also a subdued lamentation that Wanda loved right away.

She plays. Carefully. In the beginning she keeps the left pedal pushed down. She polishes her phrases, she is exact with binding the chords and her rhythm is perfect. With her hands in her lap and her head bowed, she waits for the comments from the woman in the corner.

"You play like shit. Smooth, well-adjusted, *healthy*. Like shit."

Mrs Heidelberg has gotten up and pours a waterfall of half-English, half-Dutch sentences out over Wanda. It is difficult to listen when someone has just said "like shit" to you. But the woman's genuine excitement forces Wanda to lift her head and to look at her.

"You feel something, right? This is your chance! What's going on inside your head? Show me! It makes no sense to play the piano properly. Meaningless!"

Now Wanda bends towards the keyboard, to her ivory friends. She crawls into the etude, a whispering beginning, the melody glimmers through a haze of chords melting together. The melody sounds stronger and stronger, it becomes a bitter indictment which Wanda pounds out implacably, arresting the tempo dangerously at the climax. Then dying, disappointment, finally defiant resignation.

Wanda is dizzy. From the corner Mrs Heidelberg says

softly: "Now I see what you mean. Bring me the other one next week."

Every Saturday afternoon Egbert and Emma visit Frank. In the beginning, Wanda went with them once; she remembers stench and stuffiness; she still remembers that there was a park where old parents walked around with their handi-capped children. On the way back, she threw up in the car.

"It's not a question of wanting to," says Egbert,. "You're simply going with us. You owe that to your brother."

Impatiently he stands in the hall, his coat on, holding his car keys.

"I can't. I have an engagement."

"What will you be doing?" asks Emma.

"Play trios."

"Play, play," roars Egbert. "You do nothing but play. That has to stop, you have other responsibilities and you can't keep forgetting those. You're almost eighteen!"

Forgetting, thinks Wanda. Emma used to sing a song about it: '*Glücklich ist, wer vergisst, was doch nicht zu ändern ist*', a waltz melody, light and lovely. She smiles.

"Wipe that grin off your face! And put on your coat. We're going!"

"Please, Egbert, don't force her. There's no sense in it."

Emma opens the front door and pulls her husband along. Wanda sees them go: two old people. Egbert has lost weight lately. She sees his skull beneath his skin. His cheeks are sunken. Angrily he walks around the car to unlock Emma's door.

She's no longer going to do it, Wanda decides. She'll no longer do what he says. She wants to get out. You have to start as early as possible according to Joyce. She's already in her third year and studies the violin with Mr Heidelberg. When the pianist of Joyce's trio quit, Mrs Heidelberg proposed Wanda.

"You can do it fine. Just go and practise."

She practises till she's blue in the face. Chamber music is a revelation, a wonderful game of now following and then again leading which makes Wanda think right away: this is what I want. Joyce helps her to analyse the scores and says: "You have to apply for admission. Leave that school, you have no use for it."

Lucas, the cellist, has passed his final high school examination. He doesn't get involved in the discussion. He never says anything. He has folded his long body around his cello and bows the strings in pairs with a far-away gaze in his eyes. His eyes. Wanda can't catch them, except when he looks at her, questioning, to get an A to which he can tune. During the rehearsals she has to look at his bow when they both have an entry, not at his face. His face with the wide, curved mouth and the pointed nose. His face, across which falls his hair until he shakes it back abruptly. After the rehearsal he packs up his instrument, raises his hand as a goodbye and disappears.

Joyce has brought along a registration form for Wanda. The examinations will be in a month, but the pieces that she has to play are at a level that she has already passed. She works out a programme and fills in the questionnaire. For students who are minors, a parent's signature is required. At the dinner table Wanda looks from one to the other while awaiting a good moment to say: I won't go along anymore. I'll move up to the last year of school, but I'm dropping out. You can't hold on to me, I'm leaving.

Egbert eats little. He cuts the meat into very small pieces which he chews endlessly, as if he doesn't want to swallow.

She imagines that he'll suffocate with anger if she tells them. She can't saddle Emma with it, have her justify it, have Emma stand up for her again. Then she looks so reproachful, it's just not right. She'll have to do it herself.

Egbert's signature turns out beautifully. Wanda copied it from her latest report card, and after some practising she places it at the bottom of the application form. Mrs Heidelberg signed without protest, with a little smile. "O.K. You do what you have to!"

On the day of the exam, Wanda doesn't go to school but instead to the station.

In the main concourse of The Hague there is a map. Which tram? How many stops? Look calmly, she has more than enough time. Breathe, shoulders down, take easy steps outside. And what if the tram doesn't come? Does she have enough money for a taxi? Probably not. She doesn't even see any taxis around. She has to pee. There comes the tram, fortunately.

Sit down, bag on her lap. Warm sun through the window. Sticky hands. It's taking so long before the tram starts. A bell.

Iron wheels squeak on iron rails.

Was it seven stops or eleven? Stupid, stupid, stupid to have forgotten. And how many times has the tram stopped already? Was that a stop or only a traffic light? The blouse sticks to her back, she is sweating. She'll arrive too late, much too late. She'll continue to hesitate whether to get out until the tram comes to a standstill at the final stop at the beech in Scheveningen.

She walks towards the conductor, lurching from pole to pole, and almost falls during a turn.

"Where is it?" asks the man when Wanda mentions the conservatory.

"Beestenmarkt," whispers Wanda. She has to go very badly. And she has a dry throat too, how she'd love to drink water, lots of water! At the thought of running water she can barely hold back her pee. What a long ride. Has the conductor perhaps forgotten her stop?

"Koningssingel! Get off for Beestenmarkt!"

With two feet on the traffic island. Success! Now watch out while crossing. It should be over there, on the right.

Just walk back a little and then you'll see it. A small

111

square with a large white building. The front door is open.
Next to it a sign: *Conservatory of Music.*

No one is sitting in the glass enclosure which says *Reception.*
Wanda walks past it and goes into a long hall. Cracked
slabs of pale white marble on the floor. A tall door with a
wooden sign screwed onto it: *Toilets.* She pees. Great. What
a relief. Supporting her head with two hands and her elbows
on her knees, she listens to snatches of music that come
from all directions. Through the window, the ceiling, the
pipes. Trombones, double basses, a piano far away.

Wanda sighs deeply and goes to wash her hands with
cold water, taking her time. She dries them carefully on the
inside of her skirt, she strokes every finger and rubs her
wrists, her allies.

The receptionist has returned.

"They're running overtime. They always run overtime!" he says. "Just go and have a nice cup of tea in the
cafeteria. If you go upstairs in about half an hour, you'll be
in plenty of time."

The cafeteria is a high-ceilinged room. In the corner
there is an old-fashioned stove. Wanda puts lots of sugar
in her tea and sits down on a bench against the wall. Everywhere music students sit eating and chatting. Near the stove
an older man with a music score in front of him is talking
loudly and gesturing. He is surrounded by five or so young
men who are listening to him silently.

Suddenly Wanda sees Lucas come in with a girl with
curly blond hair and a violin case in her arms. They walk

to the counter, talking intently, their heads close together.

Look at me, thinks Wanda, look!

"Hello," says Lucas. "What are you doing here?"

"Admission. In a minute."

"What are you going to play?"

"Beethoven. *Sturm.*"

"Good. You do that well. Good luck!"

Wanda walks up the creaky wooden stairs and sits down to wait on the bench near the piano room. Candidates who have already played stand whispering with their parents or their teachers. Wanda looks at no one and hears nothing. She thinks about Beethoven. Then the door swings open and a stocky man who looks vaguely familiar stands in the hall. Biermans! The pianist!

"Wanda Wiericke!" he calls out.

She stands up, smiles at him and walks slowly into the room. He closes the door behind her.

Chapter thirteen

A good car. Wanda was happy that she had a good car. Driving through the absurdly narrow streets with their sharp curves and different levels demanded, in addition to helmsmanship, especially reliable material. The houses stand right on the street here, and if you didn't watch out, you could just tear into a house and knock over a dog or a donkey.

The middle of the day and the sun at its hottest. The wheel burned in her hands. Her feet in old ladies' sandals operated the pedals with familiar ease. Three times a week she descended from her fresh airy mountaintop to the valley where the river and the road meandered together to the small city, past meadows, factory sites and campsites. It wasn't only a transition from high to low, but also one of time standing still to hours streaming along steadily, and from satisfied idleness to action.

Strange that she hadn't done anything for so long and found that rather pleasant. She'd always been busy with travelling, planning, packing suitcases, practising. Postponed rest, does that exist? As if she were catching up with all the vacations and weekends that she had missed. Just sit on a chair like last night. Look at the clouds and the sun, a slow movie. Do an errand during the day, sweep the hall with a broom, feel satisfaction when folding the clean sheets. A walk over familiar paths. Read in the *Flora* for an hour, looking for flowers that she knew. Listen to a Mozart symphony, do exercises to prevent stiffening, write a letter.

Strange that she didn't miss it, the conversations, the bustle, the meetings. She liked it fine, like this. Life had become manageable.

She parked the car in the central square and sat looking for a moment at the languid activity around her. A melon-seller sat daydreaming in his stall, a couple of tourists were selecting postcards at the newspaper stand. A woman dressed in black shuffled in the shade of the houses with a full shopping bag.

Wanda got out, locked the car and felt the hot sun on her head and her arms. Everywhere water was gurgling, three rivers came together here. In addition the soil was full of boiling-hot, sulphur-containing spring water that since time immemorial had squirted out at the strangest places in the city. The water had made the city famous and gave it a great head start in the competition with other spas. More springs, higher temperatures, more therapeutic minerals.

Wanda had fallen for it. On a cold autumn day she had driven through the valley to the parking place where she stood now. At the end of the square hung a strange cloud of steam or mist; curious she had strolled towards it. An enormous square basin had been sunk into the ground with three continuous stair treads around it. On the lowest tread sat people who had pulled up their trousers or their skirts and had put their shoes next to them. They kept their feet in the water and gazed out peacefully. Some held conversations in soft voices, and then fell silent again. Without thinking Wanda had sat down on the upper tread, had taken off her shoes and socks and had lowered herself. The hot water stung her calves, she pulled her legs up and tried it again, now slowly. Her feet found support on the smooth stone bottom. From two corners of the basin fresh water streamed in; in the other corners grates had been installed through which the water could run off. The difference between her cold cheeks and her hot feet was pleasant in an odd way. The water stank incredibly; above the healing spring hung a penetrating smoke of sulphur and sewer gases. She let her eyes move slowly over the buildings next to the hospital. A medieval hospital, rebuilt into a rehabilitation institute behind the old façades. Patients drove or tottered through the archway. They pushed walkers or crutches aside and lowered their legs into the water. A sturdy nurse came outside with a towel over her arm to help someone back out again. In the wall of the church on the square, a niche had been built around a fountain. Spluttering and hissing, a thick stream of steaming water splattered into a basin. Now and then someone came by, filled a bucket and then disappeared again in the drizzle.

Wanda stripped off her gloves and stuck her hands into the water next to her knees, the painful thumb joints, the slightly swollen wrists. An old gentlemen across the way nodded at her, smiling.

After half an hour she had stood up as if reborn; she almost lost her footing on the slippery stone but was able to balance herself again fast. She had immediately gone to look for a real estate agent.

She was a regular customer in the stately grey bath house at the edge of the city, a building from the beginning of the previous century, set in a shady park with tall, exotic trees and a never-used bandstand. After her spa appointment she liked to walked around there, she never met anyone and the nitrous fumes could peacefully evaporate in the always cool air. The whole complex lay wedged between the steeply rising rock wall and the river.

The façade had fallen into disrepair: rusted hinges on the shutters and peeling paint on the woodwork. Behind the front door everything was new. There were glass linen cupboards filled with towels and bathrobes of waffle-weave cloth; polished marble benches stuck out of the walls, and chrome steel handrails had been installed along all walkways. The staff members, even the doctors who had sold their souls to this house, were dressed in light blue, the patients in white. At the desk a fat woman of about sixty was sneaking a cigarette. She snapped at two tourists who had slipped in out of curiosity but welcomed Wanda warmly.

"Pfff! On the door it says: by appointment. Only on medical grounds. Here you are, madam, towel, bathrobe, and may I have your card?"

She carefully stamped the card, laid the gear on the counter and shook Wanda's hand.

All those conversations with people, in her awkward French, were not for her, she had always hated and avoided them. Now she actually thought it was nice. Wanda in a thermal spa! Delivering herself to these frauds in their light-blue coats, subjecting herself to their water cures which she knew had to be quackery or drivel. Not for her – and look at her now!

She undressed in the small cubicle and threw the bathrobe around her. On plastic slippers she started the shuffling trip through the establishment like all the other patients.

Old people, men with surprisingly thin legs under expansive stomachs, women whose skulls shone through their wet hair, people with swollen feet, rheumatic hands, bent spinal columns, stiff necks, pain, pain, pain. They walked at a leisurely pace from the doctor's office to the showers and the masseuse. They'd have a chat, ask how things were today, how the night had been, what the plans were for Sunday. Over everything hung an acoustic blanket of hissing, splashing and gurgling. And the smell of sulphur.

Finally she ended up in the bathroom, alone. The bath was filled to the brim with freshly drawn sulphur water, set in motion by an air-powered system. She climbed into it and lowered herself backwards. Streams of water beat against her bottom, back and thighs. The temperature was exactly right. You could fall asleep, the sounds blended into a pleasant whole, restful, reassuring, healing. The sounds no longer demanded to be converted into their elements, you could take them in their context, you could let yourself float in the volcanic stink-soup from the bowels of the earth and let your ears be filled with that thick murmur.

Fleetingly she thought of the misery of analysing; how at the beginning of her professional training she had been alarmed because she could no longer hear a piece of music without paying attention to the form, waiting for the return of the theme, hearing the modulations and where they went. What had moved her had become practice material. She no longer really loved music, she had thought, she could no longer feel it, only understand it.

The love had returned. During the third or the fourth year of her studies she could again listen and be moved. And now, decades later, she could hear Haydn, Mozart and Schubert again. For pleasure. No Brahms, scarcely any Bach, no chamber music and especially no piano works, but instead symphonies for string orchestra with a few wind players.

She smiled. It is a baby-feeling to just lie in the moving, warm water, in the smell, in the diffuse noise. No joint hurts any more, no movement is difficult. You could stay here until the skin soaked off your bones in greyish flaps; utterly trusting, you would let yourself disintegrate and be washed down the drain.

That's why they have stern young women working here, thought Wanda, naked in the water. Young women with black hair, made-up faces and shrill voices. They come in abruptly, let the door bang against the wall so that the lock jingles, they tear the stopper out of the bath, turn off the bubble machine and scream that time's up.

Chapter fourteen

The cello case stands next to the door like a dark watchman. Wanda can't sleep any longer, she lies on her side looking into her room. There is only one orderly spot: the cabinet with music. Mr De Leon's inheritance lies in a system of stacks waiting to be performed. Music has to lie flat, otherwise the backs sag. In front of the cabinet glasses are standing on the floor, a half-empty wine bottle, a full ashtray. In the middle of the room she sees her black performance dress, half hidden by trousers and a wrinkled shirt, on the sloppily painted floor boards. Over the desk chair hangs a dress suit. Next to her lies Lucas Lansingh. Black hair, a naked shoulder, a curve under the blanket. Wanda doesn't dare to move for fear that he'll wake up. She lies on the edge of the mattress, an arm and a leg on the floor. She breathes carefully.

Last night Brahms. For the very well-attended evening performance, the cello-piano duo had been planned as the last piece of the programme. "We're not going to sit in the audience," Lucas had said. "I don't want to listen to all that junk. Come. We're going to warm up a little in room fourteen, upstairs."

While he unpacked and polished his instrument clean, Wanda did her exercises and a scale in octaves, in E minor. They played a piece of each part, for the tempo. They talked about their positions. "Face me," she had said, "not the audience. At least half-way towards me. I have to see you."

Wanda loves this sonata with a mystifying passion. Even the last part, the fugue with the relentless accumulation of triplets. The way Lucas plays, how their voices interweave, turn around each other, sometimes as if in a dance, sometimes as if in a joust— she treasures all that. When she thinks about the trio of the middle movement she feels her throat swell with tenderness, with inexpressible, disappointed hope. She thinks that he feels it too; his mouth is contorted when he plays, he looks like an unapproachable, deeply wounded hero.

The audience had cheered. Afterwards they drank wine in the cafeteria. When Lucas got ready to leave, Wanda put on her coat as well. They walked next to each other in the wet street. She was dizzy from the alcohol and the success, and she held her warm face up to the raindrops. He had thrown his free arm around her shoulders. Why? Her thoughts raced ahead excitedly: a mess in her room, dirty sheets, the bed not made.

Later, sprawling on the mattress, they had drunk more bad red wine. Then he had put his long muscled cello hands around her face. He had kissed her thoughtfully. She had let herself be kissed like a small child. Through her head raced shreds of questions: is he in love with me, why does he do this, how will it end? They had made love by the light of a candle. With closed eyes he had come into her and had groaned in her neck. She had screamed and then cried. Why? Afterward he wanted to go home but he fell asleep suddenly.

Light comes from under the curtain. She has to get up, she stinks, fluid runs along the inside of her thighs. The bathroom is at the end of the hall, across from the kitchen. Wanda turns on the shower to its fullest, its hottest. When she comes back, Lucas has disappeared.

She sits down on the floor to reflect. Only go to bed with someone if you love him very much. Be careful that you don't get pregnant. She blushes at the thought of her carelessness. Let yourself be carried away like that, it's dangerous, don't do it again. But he, can't he watch out too? They made love in the same way that they play. With dedication and total commitment. And afterwards back home or to school, as if nothing has happened. Does she want to go on with Lucas? She is only afraid that she'll do something that he won't like. She can't say anything to him. She doesn't dare to ask him anything.

It's another kind of awkwardness than with Peter, who

sometimes comes to eat with her and keeps staring at her with his friendly face. Wanda went to bed with him a few times, out of pity, because she no longer knew what to say, because she didn't know how to handle his faithful devotion. During the act she had the feeling that she was standing next to the bed looking at herself. Afterwards she avoided him and refused his invitations.

The last time he had said that they shouldn't do it anymore, it wasn't right, she didn't know what she wanted anyway, it would be better for them not to see each other. He had looked sad but Wanda was relieved. She looks at the small piano next to the music cabinet. Practising won't work now. She is so full, full of something that should come out in words, not in the elusive language of music. Words, but which ones? She has always had a weary disdain for them. Now she'd really like a long talk.

Wanda rings at Joyce's door. Actually you can't go and visit music students because they always have to practise. Necessity knows no law on this windy morning. Joyce will say so if it doesn't suit her. I have to be with someone, it's impossible like this. Joyce has put her violin in the case and starts to make coffee. She rubs a painful red spot under her chin.

"Have you recovered yet from yesterday? Brilliantly played. You two are very well matched, a strong duo."

"He stayed." Limply Wanda sinks down in the only chair.

"Here's your coffee," says Joyce. "I'm putting it on

the floor. You shouldn't fall in love with Lucas. He can't stand to be tied down and he can't stand companionship. I've known him for so long. He truly is a conductor. You shouldn't tie yourself to him, you'll be destroyed."

Joyce is taking her final examinations this year. She is twenty-five years old and she knows everything. She also has a fiancé who works at a newspaper. She doesn't understand and Wanda can't explain. Wanda has such a yearning, such an excessive hunger, but for what? She'd better not count on others. She should just study.

During the weekend she can't be at school and can't stand to be in her room. She gets on the train to visit her parents. Egbert reconciled himself quickly to Wanda's choice of profession when he realized that her refusal to take the final high school examination was serious. He pays her a monthly allowance and gave her the practice piano. To her surprise, Wanda noticed that she didn't like his quick capitulation. Should he have objected, had she wanted to fight? If he thinks that education is so important, why doesn't he force her to study law? It seems as if he suddenly doesn't care anymore. What she does leaves him cold.

She shakes off those thoughts. Nonsense. He can't be *that* indifferent. Maybe he understood that it has to be like that. Biermans spoke with him after the entrance exam. Maybe they had a disagreement and Biermans won. That child was born to play the piano, Mr Wiericke. That's what you think, Mr Biermans, but I'm responsible and I won't let her go. But you owe it to art. Oh, all right then.

Wanda grins. It could not have gone like that; Egbert doesn't quarrel with instructors at respectable institutions. He let Emma do the talking and resigned himself to the decision that was taken.

Something is wrong in the house. Something has changed, but no matter how she looks around she sees no difference from the past. The same furniture, the same wallpaper, familiar objects. Still. Maybe there's something wrong with her. She no longer looks at things in the same way. Emma asks about her study. When Wanda tells her about the lessons, the choir class and the evening performance, she sees that her mother is absently staring at her hands. She looks tired and is wearing an old cardigan. Wanda doesn't dare to ask what is wrong.

Dinner is ready and Egbert comes out of his study. Wanda walks towards him. Through the open door she sees that there is a sofa in the study. That's new. She gives Egbert a kiss. He smells strange. The three of them eat in the kitchen. Egbert has become thinner again, his neck has folds and his shirt-collar is much too loose.

Wanda wonders why she is here. Because she's in love. Because she's alone. Because she's confused. Because they have to take care of her. But they're not in the mood for that.

"What's the matter with you two?"

"Your father is sick," says Emma. "There is something wrong with his throat. He can barely eat."

"Can you go to your work?" Wanda asks Egbert.

"Only for administrative matters," he whispers. "I tire quickly. I can't talk very easily."

Wanda feels inclined to start whispering too but forces herself to speak normally. She clears her throat.

"Do you know what it is?"

Egbert and Emma look at each other.

"No," says Emma. "Doctor Tromp has referred us to a specialist; we're going there next week."

After the meal Egbert lies down. Wanda and Emma hear him coughing in his room.

"Has it been like this for a long time?" asks Wanda.

"He doesn't like to be sick, your father. For a long time he acted as if nothing was the matter. But now he has difficulty speaking, now people notice it and say something about it. That he has to go to the doctor. He didn't want to at first."

"But he doesn't speak. He doesn't *eat*."

"That's why he's going now."

Wanda decides that it's better to say nothing. If she says that she feels lost without Lucas, is it true? When Joyce said that he was unreliable, he really became that way. Now she's in love because she has thought that word. Actually she only wants to study and play, and make all words unsaid and unthought.

Egbert undergoes treatment in the hospital and his symptoms decrease. He is able to eat better and his voice has more volume. The nature of the illness is not discussed. And Wanda doesn't ask about it either. She studies. She accompanies Lucas during his final cello-examination and doesn't speak about what has happened between them, doesn't think that she'd like to kick in his instrument and sit between his knees herself, doesn't think at all except about Beethoven opus 69, A major.

After the examination, Lucas throws himself into training to be a conductor. He walks around with a bag filled with orchestra scores. When Wanda puts on any record, he can tell after two minutes which conductor is standing in front of the orchestra.

"I don't understand that you don't want to play yourself," says Wanda. "To make your own sound, isn't that the most beautiful thing?"

"No, that's ballast," says Lucas. "To have a whole orchestra in your head and then move in such a way that they will do what *you* hear. That's the most beautiful."

He practises in front of the mirror. Every Friday morning he stands in front of the conservatory orchestra. In the Mozart year he is going to conduct the festival programme. Wanda is the soloist. He stands next to the grand piano when she plays and beats the air. They talk about tempos and dynamics, just like before.

"It's a shame that boy is going to conduct," thinks Biermans. "An excellent cellist. The way you played that Brahms sonata at the time, that was class."

"But he's good," protests Wanda.

"My dear, listen to your teacher: conducting has one

great advantage – it makes no sound. It's you who'll have to do that."

On the day of the concert Wanda is nervous. That's not an unpleasant feeling. The nerves give tension and a goal to the day. Thinking ahead doesn't go past the final chord. Then there is black silence.

She prepares for the performance as if it were a date with a lover whom she hasn't seen for a long time. A long shower. Cuts her nails. Chooses underwear that fits perfectly and matches well. Light make-up, only some mascara and eye shadow because she'll sweat and wipe her face. An agreeable awareness of her body, the whole day. Doesn't eat too much. Has a good crap. In the morning practises for a solid hour and a half, after that a little technique from time to time, very minimally. Quietly sits on a chair and reads through the whole score. The music is Mr De Leon's, his name is on the crumbling paper of the cover. Although she knows the concerto by heart from beginning to end, she takes the book along when she goes to the conservatory at the end of the afternoon, together with the apple and the dress and the handkerchief in her bag.

The large hall is decorated with dark red drapes with portraits of Mozart attached here and there. On the podium Lucas practises with the orchestra the symphony that will be played before the intermission. He is wearing an old, checked shirt. He lets the winds play chords and gives indications for the intonation. Before the winds become noisy, he ends the rehearsal. He turns around and sees Wanda standing in the aisle. Eye to eye.

The most difficult period is the time before intermission. Wanda has to concentrate on her solo concerto while the symphony is being played on the stage. The junk room behind the stage is the dressing-room. In it stand enormous basses, a harp, broken kettledrums and boxes with orchestra material. She has peed three times, has put on her black dress and has washed her hands. Now she circles through the storeroom while drying her fingers one after the other with a dish towel. Applause. Noise of the audience stumbling out. Lucas comes in with two bottles of mineral water. He grins. He looks happy.

130   The auditorium starts filling again. Through a crack in the covered back of the stage, Wanda and Lucas look into the hall. He has thrown his arms around her and presses his chin into her hair. They rock back and forth in the tempo of the first part, with the syncopations and the ominous chords that come rolling closer.

Emma and Egbert come in! They sit down in the last row, on the middle aisle. Egbert has a cane which Emma places against the wall behind their chairs. The orchestra climbs onto the stage. There is tuning. Then it is quiet.

Lucas conducts an impassioned, wild Mozart with great dynamic differences and strong accents. He gives the concerto a desperate tragic feeling which doesn't become ridiculous because he allows neither players nor listeners any distance from the music. In the hall rages a storm that touches and sweeps everyone along. God-like, Lucas reigns over vessel and elements; he is able to control the outbursts just in time and contains the orchestra sound to a whisper before every piano entry. Wanda holds the conversation with him that is never possible in words. She no longer thinks of her teacher, nor of the cloud of envy that hangs above her co-students, nor of her parents in the last row. She conforms to Lucas' melody, she takes over and forces the orchestra to listen. She storms and sings and chisels while not forgetting for a moment where she wants to take back the tempo, where the important modulation comes, at which place the arm muscles have to relax for a moment. Her brain is so wide open that all these matters fit into it effortlessly. After the final chord she stays seated for a minute, as if stunned.

"I take it back," says Biermans while clinking his glass against Wanda's. "That friend of yours has it. Yes, of course you can't play Mozart like that at all, it's a violation. But he compels it, he does it. All my respect! And for you too, my girl. I listened to you with pleasure. Where are your parents? I thought I saw them sitting in the hall?"

"They left again. My father is ill. They wanted to go home."

During the drumming applause she had seen Egbert's back bend. The coughing fit couldn't be heard but she saw that Emma took the cane, pulled a handkerchief from her pocket and gently pushed her husband out of the hall.

Wanda and Lucas stood hand in hand in front of the grand piano and bowed stiffly. They squeezed each other's hands hard and Wanda knew: tonight he stays with me.

*

An expanding growth in the oesophagus, the doctor had said. Still Wanda hadn't found the right word until the doorman pointed her to the oncology department. Cancer. So that's what it is. His throat is pressed shut by a growing tumour. Food cannot get through and words can no longer get out. In the elevator she stands with her hands around her neck. He will suffocate. Nothing can be done about it.

132   Egbert has a fever. Drops of sweat stand on his forehead and he seems confused. He slumps half upright in the high hospital bed and looks at Wanda without recognizing her. This is my father, she thinks. He is angry and can no longer express it. Does he know that his life is ending? Maybe he has regrets. Regrets about the war, about Frankie, about her. Things haven't gone the way he wanted. She doesn't know him; she doesn't know what he's thinking. She has to sit down next to him and talk to him. If only Emma would come.

She pulls a stool over next to his bed and takes his hand.

"Do you want to drink? Are you thirsty?"

Egbert shakes his head no. He looks at Wanda with

glaring eyes. From his throat comes a noise. He yanks away his hand. Wanda's eyes fill with tears from shock and discomfort. Egbert points with his hand to the table near the window. Then his head droops to the side and he nods off for a moment.

If only Emma would come now. She can't face this. She thought he'd be happy to see her. The idea! After all, when you're suffocating you don't want whining children around you who don't do what you want. Then you want air. Wanda goes into the hall. Behind the desk sits a nurse who looks at her in a friendly way.

"I don't quite know what to do," Wanda says to her. "He's disgruntled, but why?"

"I'll take a look. He's a bit confused today, it's a bad day."

The nurse is about two years older than Wanda and knows exactly what to do. She's not afraid. She takes Egbert's shoulders gently. She wets his lips with a wash cloth and wipes the sweat from his forehead. She looks under the sheets quickly to make sure that the gruesome tubes still function properly. She places a hand on Egbert's cheek and looks at him while she speaks.

"Mr Wiericke! Could you write down what you want?"

She pulls a small notebook from her apron pocket and puts a pen in Egbert's hand. Egbert's arm trembles. With difficulty he draws a letter on the paper. It's a W.

But when Wanda comes towards him again, he shakes his head and pushes her away with his arm. With the letter

in her hand, she sits down in the hall. A phrase nags at her:
he wants me but he doesn't want me.

With her coat hanging open, Emma steps out of the elevator. Her heels tap on the floor. She sits down on the bench
next to Wanda. She smells of home.

"Just look at this," says Wanda. "The nurse asked
what he wanted and then he wrote this. The W of Wanda.
But he didn't want to see me at all, he pushed me away."

"He means Mr Winter. From the pharmacy. A friend
of his. I think that he's the one he wants to speak to."

"Oh," says Wanda.

Emma starts to cry.

"He no longer wants to live. And it's terrible. They
no longer do anything. Yes, wait till he dies."

Wanda doesn't know what to say. She feels an intense
shame. The W of Wanda, of Wretched, of Wrong-headed,
that's what he meant. The W of Wasted. And of Worthless.

"Why do you let me come then if no one needs me?"
Wanda gets up and paces up and down in front of her
mother. "Did you think that was nice for me? I don't want
this, you hear! I can't do it and I don't want it."

"He has an understanding," Emma says softly, "an
understanding with Winter. He supplies the medicines so
that he – oh well, will fall asleep. They discussed this long
ago."

"And you knew that?"

"Of course I knew that. I was there."

Emma blows her nose.

"Why do you never tell me anything? Why don't I know what's going on? I come here and look like a fool because no one tells me anything!"

Sometimes it's better not to know things, Emma had said. They mean well, she mustn't be so loud. Not be so selfish.

*

Chopin's twenty-four preludes are not loose impressions accidentally thrown together between two covers; in many ways they form a coherent whole that means more to Wanda than the sum of the parts.

"Go ahead and do that," says Biermans, "it's a good choice."

There is going to be a recording for a radio series in which various famous pianists introduce one of their students. Wanda was chosen by her teacher and she wants to play the preludes, all of them. He doesn't ask why; she wouldn't be able to say. Vaguely, at a distance, she feels that this work has something to do with protest, with a raging complaint about inevitable injustice. Or with almost nonchalantly waving aside a catastrophic destiny. Something to do with death, too. As if you let yourself float away with death – and in the next prelude you deny everything that has happened. She doesn't need the words. She practises.

"Radio is demanding," says Biermans. "You have no public. If something goes wrong it can be done again, you think.

You sit in one of these sound-proof cabins without windows. You hear yourself breathe. You see little lights everywhere. Behind the wall are guys with earphones on their heads. You can see them, through a small window, but you don't know if they hear you when you say something. These are exasperating circumstances."

Wanda laughs. She acts as if Biermans is a recording device and plays through the whole cycle. Then the lesson is almost over. When it is quiet she hears that traffic noises penetrate from the street. The lamp hums. Wanda sits motionless, and Biermans walks to the piano. While she played, he sat in a corner of the room. Now he stands in the curve of the grand piano and, leaning on the casing, he bends towards her.

"The way you hold everything together by tuning all these twenty-four pieces to each other, every musician with ears on his head will be jealous of that. Me too. It's a gift that you should always preserve. The secret of Wanda Wiericke. Keep it safe."

Wanda understands what he's talking about and nods at him, smiling. Biermans continues to speak. "Now I'll tell you Biermans' secret. When I listen to you like this I think: Chopin sweeps her along. Maybe she's even thinking about her dead father. Any minute things will get out of hand. She feels too much. There's nothing against that, it's good. *But!!* Underneath that feeling there must be a second layer, a safety-net which is always there. You are crocheting that safety-net when you practise. At every chord, at every phrase you know: now I'm going to do this, now I'm going to throw my arm joint into it, now only fingers, now play towards the next measure, hold back so that the next accent will be marked, relax the wrist, etcetera. You have to translate everything you feel into technique. When you play you have to be bilingual. A person who can play only in the technical language may be a virtuoso but dull. A person who plays only in the language of feeling is expressive but undisciplined. The secret is bilingualism. If you combine that with your own secret, no listener will be able to turn off the radio."

Wanda nods. She strokes the ivory of the keys. He is right. He says it well. But is it as simple, as uncomplicated as he pictures it? It is true, but is that all? And her own secret as he calls it, what should she do with it? She doesn't know her own secret but yet she knows what he means.

Wanda gets up. She shakes Biermans' hand and leaves the classroom. Outside the sun beats down on her bare arms. Egbert has died and Wanda studies the preludes.

Chapter fifteen

Carefully she steered the car up the mountain, letting up on the gas at every turn. She could still have had a drink on the square, walked along the streams, looked around at the old bathhouse in the centre of town, done some errands. She didn't do it. She was on her way home and in fifteen minutes she would walk in.

In the late afternoon the mountains looked regal. Blue-black crests were outlined sharply against the yellowish sky. On the treeless meadow the horses stood close together. Their skins shone like a just-varnished violin. A farmer with a bale of hay on his neck trudged to the barn, a girl in a faded blue dress was cutting roses in the garden, and from the village chimneys smoke was rising. Wanda was aware of everything. Her pain was gone.

She should have a good meal for once, perhaps in the hotel? With soup before and wine with it. A wave of nausea struck though stomach and throat. She squeezed her hands firmly around the steering wheel. Her arms trembled. On getting out she noticed that her knees could not be trusted. She remained standing for a moment, leaning against the grey wall of the house. The warmth of the stones penetrated her back and she rested her head against the doorpost.

The thing. The black monster. The room was a stage that she had to enter. She had to go and sit at the grand piano and everything would turn black.

"There, there," said Biermans, "you look as if you expect to be murdered. Believe me, the end of time is not yet near."

Behind the stage Wanda waited until the hall was quiet. She was working on her fear. Bug off, she thought when her teacher came in. What's it to you, keep your pep talk to yourself, go away, go away. She straightened her back and looked at her hands with the trembling fingers that lay pale against the black fabric of her dress. The anger gave her strong legs on which she walked resolutely to her instrument.

It wasn't discussed at school. A real musician had no fear, and whoever was afraid should consider another profession. You need a little tension, Biermans had said when Wanda dared to broach the subject one time. It sharpens your senses, that's good. You shouldn't fret about it, that only makes it worse. If need be, you just pretend that you're sitting at home in your study. And no one will eat you, the people sitting in the auditorium are civilized.

Annoyed, she began to play. There were people who had abandoned their career because they almost died of fright before every concert. In the last minute before coming on the stage it was war. You had to go onto the field of battle, you couldn't back out. Not all soldiers are equally brave. She had even heard Lucas puke in the toilet behind the stage. He looked pale when he reappeared and had knocked away her hand when she wanted to caress him. A talented oboist talked to himself, aloud: you *can* do it you *can* do it! Startled, Wanda slid between the curtains so that he couldn't see her. Whether you could play or not made no difference. Everyone was afraid.

Without consulting anyone she had constructed a routine which was fairly reliable. All day the performance hovered in the background of her thoughts, from the first morning diarrhoea until the heroic trip to the stage. Clothes were important. A dress with wide sleeves of the kind of fabric on which you could wipe your hands if necessary. Not too revealing, that gave such an unprotected feeling at your back. The upper arms have to be covered. The worst was straps falling down. Wanda had a solid concert bra.

High heels, a cellist had said. Then you feel yourself standing above it all, it gives support! Next to a cello tall legs look lively, but on the piano pedals high heels don't have a chance. You could perhaps enter the stage on them and then hide them under your full skirt. But how do you get

them back on when the applause starts? Wanda had flats
with thin soles through which she could feel the metal of
the pedals. She imagined being tall by holding her neck
and back straight above the tightened buttocks.

"Are you never nervous?" she asked Joyce after a trio
rehearsal.

"I just die. Agonies! Especially when I have to wait,
when the piano has two pages before I begin. Or when the
piece starts softly and slowly, then my bow shakes and you
can *hear* it. Terrible."

"I've never noticed it," said Wanda. "Do you have a
method? What do you do for it?"

Joyce turns bright red. She has clamped her left hand
around her right wrist and sucks on her middle finger.

"I can't tell you. I'm so embarrassed."

Suddenly Wanda felt her cheeks sting too.

"Does it help?"

"It doesn't always work. You have to be alone some-
place. Recently I was in the toilet behind the stage and
Bella Heidelberg started banging on the door, checking if
I was ready! Then it didn't work. But *when* it works: yes."

Wanda tore herself away from the wall and unlocked the
front door of her house. She didn't have to. She could sit
at the kitchen table with the paper, with a glass of wine;
she could leave the room closed. It was over, she never had
to again.

Never again slowly into the light. Slower than you

wanted to towards the white keyboard. Sit down deliberately. Feel, look. Look into the hall. It was not a study, there were rows upon rows of people waiting for sound. Always, against the back wall leaned that one, in dark clothes, the hat making a shadow on his face. Always that one for whom she played.

Chapter sixteen

P anting, Wanda pushes open the heavy door. The drops that she shakes from her coat spatter on the marble of the hallway. Her shoes clatter on the wooden staircase. She's late, very late, in the large hall the ensemble is already set up, the microphones have been placed, the positions determined and Gilles, who takes care of the sound engineering, sits behind the recording device.

He looks up for a moment when Wanda enters. The stage is empty, the musicians sit facing it. It must have been a lot of work to clear away all the chairs. Wanda puts her coat on a stack of chairs next to the door and pulls the loose sheets of her part from her coat pocket. She remains standing for a moment until Lucas taps his baton and the sounds stop. Then she steps forward. Lucas points to the grand piano, squeezed between a group of violists and a percussion battery. She comes for him. For the rest she has no business here. Last year Wanda took her final examination and now is studying for her soloist diploma. The weekly lessons with Biermans are her only obligation. In addition she has her ensemble and performs from time to time. She stands with one foot in the real world and through Lucas she keeps informed about what is happening in the conservatory. There is a new director, a composer. For the first time instead of a Rachmaninov, a work by Ton de Leeuw was played at the final performance. The ink was still wet.

In the following summer some students went to Cologne to work in the new electronic studio. They came back with scores by Stockhausen and Varèse; they pressed instrumentalists to learn these works and organized concerts with the approval of the board. During that same summer Wanda went to Salzburg for a Beethoven course.

Over the years Schönberg and Stravinsky had become familiar to her, but she was shocked when Lucas took her with him to a rehearsal of the newest music. He was enthusiastic; there was renewed life in the composition class. The students were influenced by the new idiom and he liked conducting their damned difficult products. When he was presented with a piece with a hard piano part, he approached Wanda.

Lucas stands behind a rectangular drawing table. On it lies the score. On a stool next to him sits the composer who is called Tsjak but who formerly, when he still was a timid piano student, was called Erik-Jan. Wanda still remembers that he was so shy in solfège class that he didn't dare to sing and always blushed when it was his turn. Now he wears tight pants with suspenders; his hair is cut short and stands straight up above the boyish face.

Lucas winks at Wanda when she takes her seat. He looks at his watch.

"Tonight we'll get it together. Meanwhile Gilles will check the sound. Next week we'll record it in one sitting, at night, when the trams have stopped running. I'd now like everyone at the letter Q."

An inconceivable ruckus breaks out. Wanda has difficulty discerning any kind of rhythm in it. She's glad that Lucas indicates the start of each measure clearly with a large downward arm motion. It is a restless composition without silences.

145

They take a long break. Gilles has brought a tray with coffee from the cafeteria. He takes it to a group of girls dressed in black, with straight hair and black-rimmed eyes. One after the other they take a cup from the tray. No sugar, no milk.

"It's such a difficult part," a violist says to Wanda. "And you don't hear anything of it. We sit bowing like fools. Gilles! Why can't we be heard?"

When Gilles comes closer, Wanda sees the scars on his face. A one-time pimple-face on an enormous body. Gilles is a percussionist and leader of the ensemble that is called The Future.

"Be heard? That's not the purpose."

"What?" says Wanda. "I've worked myself to death. It's very complicated. And not very pianistically written, if I may say so."

Gilles sniffs. "You have to get it. What Tsjak creates. Can't be explained. New work."

Wanda doesn't understand it. She doesn't understand these people. How they think about music. She must know more about it, then she might start to appreciate it. That's how it goes with new music. When you know the sequence of notes, when you get used to the succession of chords, then there comes a day that you are attached to it and like it. She'll try it once more.

"If the sound balance is so distorted, then the listeners can't find it beautiful either, can they?"

Gilles sticks his large hands in the pockets of his trousers. Unmoved, he looks at Wanda.

"Do you care about beautiful? Then you don't understand it at all. That's what I thought. I saw you at it. Terribly aesthetic. It looks like you're playing the piano! No, you're infected with the performers' disease. You'll never get it."

The violist has walked away. Wanda doesn't know what to do.

"And Lucas?"

"Lucas is OK. He feels it. He's behind us. Lucas isn't in love with beauty."

Wanda looks around. Where is Lucas? He's standing next to Tsjak, they are looking at the gigantic score. Lucas' hand lies on the boyish neck of the composer. With his thumb he rubs the short hairs. Tsjak looks up at Lucas, smiles. Lucas pushes his hip against the boy's thin body and smiles back.

Oh, thinks Wanda. Oh.

Gilles has walked over to his sound box and the string players are chattering together in a corner. Wanda grabs her coat and slips out of the door.

How should she say it? Are you keen on that boy, how can it be that you do it with me as well? How does that work, I don't understand it. Explain it to me.

They sit across from each other at a table in the cafeteria. Wanda's voice sounds unusually vehement.

"You sell yourself to these guys! Only because you can make radio recordings. It's not fair!"

"Well," says Lucas, "I like the fact that attention is being paid to it. I can't deny that."

"That you make yourself available for that stupid music! I think it's a betrayal."

Yes, he's a traitor and a fraud. Wanda's cheeks are red and her eyes glitter.

"You see that all wrong," Lucas says cautiously. "These guys are trying to create something new. Repudiating normal beauty – I can appreciate that."

"And what about Brahms? You're lying!"

"Yes. Brahms. I'm a conductor, I try everything. Else you're nowhere."

"But they can't do anything. It's gibberish what they create. You *know* that, Lucas, don't you?"

"Yes. No. You're right in a certain sense. But also not. You have to think about it. You're lying in an age-old bed. Shouldn't we get up, shouldn't something new be coming? At least those boys are trying!"

She doesn't say what she wants to say, she can't. How do men do it with each other? And does he think of her then?

Lucas has risen to his feet. He raises his hand and leaves the cafeteria.

*

The next morning Wanda takes the train home on an impulse. Everywhere she sees people who are on their way, who carry along bags and paperwork. People who are awaited by others, who have to be on time somewhere and have a conversation, take up a post and fill an emptiness. Wanda's hands lie on her lap.

The travellers disperse in the main concourse. Rushed and resolute they stride towards their goal with their bags under their arms. The doors of stores and offices stand open to let in the workers. In her coat pocket Wanda is holding the key to her mother's house. The wind has swept the leaves off the trees along the Singel. The endless road over the bridge with its scary rescue-hook, past the half-drowned willow and the ducks is travelled in no time.

"Mum! I'm home!"

In the entrance hall hangs a strange coat, an enormous cloak with a collar of flat, curly fur. Wanda hangs her own coat over a kitchen chair and sits down at the table. In the garden the brown stalks of sunflowers and marguerites stick out above a carpet of fallen leaves.

Make coffee, look in the refrigerator. In it lie a couple of slender bottles of white wine between packages from the cheese store. Salted butter. Sour cream. Venison steak. Wanda hears bumping on the stairs, shuffling on the stone floor of the hall, the click of the front door – or is she imagining that? Emma enters in her bathrobe.

"Darling, what a surprise! Did something happen for you to come so early? I wasn't even out of bed yet!"

The skin of Emma's face is smoother and more filled out than it used to be. Her hair shines. She sits relaxed across from Wanda and smiles. The bathrobe falls open and she ties it up. She's wearing nothing underneath.

"I haven't been here in such a long time. I didn't feel like practising. Some rehearsals were cancelled, I have time."

"If only you'd called I would have got up and picked up something for you. Will you do that next time? You caught me somewhat unawares."

She should get dressed, thinks Wanda. She should fix her hair like she used to and there should be normal food in the house, milk and bread and a big piece of young cheese.

While Emma dresses, Wanda goes to the bakery with the straw shopping bag. The coat has disappeared.

"I've started singing again, yes. It started with the light opera society, their lead suddenly had a hernia, and the understudy couldn't handle the part. Then they asked me and I said yes. I thought: I'll just see how I like it. I can always change my mind. I found it wonderful, just *won*der-ful. As if I'd come home. I've started practising again and I give lessons. Ten students and more are coming. The strange thing is that I'm not tired, while I do much more than before. I'm also starting to appear professionally again: morning concerts, duets and lieder. With Bella Heidelberg, what do you think of *that!*"

"And those duets?"

"A baritone. A very beautiful, dark voice. He's from Belgium."

Emma blushes. She gets up and rummages in the kitchen drawer, looking for knives that are already on the table.

150   After breakfast Wanda escapes the warm kitchen to walk through the polder. The wind blows tears over her cheeks. In the familiar meadows, houses are being built and parks laid out. Everything is becoming different and better, she thinks, even my mother. I don't belong at home anymore, not in this city and not in this house. Emma is happy, she is singing again; Wanda should be glad for her.

A bundle of Schubert lieder stands open on the grand piano. Brahms lies on top of a stack of operetta scores and voice exercises next to the music stand. Wanda plays her scales. Quickly try Schubert; immediately Emma sings along from the kitchen. Drying her hands on a dishtowel, she comes and stands behind the piano. Her voice has become a little worn and in the high notes it has acquired an edge that wasn't there before. The phrasing is flawless, the finish is polished and an unrestrained pleasure sounds through everything Emma sings.

That's how it should be, thinks Wanda, the two of us making music like long ago, before all the others came in between. Would she be thinking of *him* now that she's performing with a pianist again? She sings the same songs and hears the same accompaniment. She must think of him, only by always thinking of the dead can you keep them with you. But of course she thinks only of that Belgian, of venison steak and matinée programmes.

The bell rings and Emma flies off, leaving the dish-towel behind on the piano. Wanda follows her into the hall, slowly and deliberately.

Framed by a wild autumn sky, a heavily-built man stands in the doorway. He is wearing the coat with the flattened fur collar and extends his hand to Wanda.

"Guido de Bock. And you are the famous daughter. The pianist!"

Sausage fingers and an overwhelming, warm voice. A friendly laugh. A nice man. He hangs his coat on the coat hook himself and rubs Emma's back as they walk to the kitchen. They drink tea. He asks about Wanda's experiences at the conservatory, wants to know what she likes to play and which pianists she likes. A nice man.

"We were just singing," says Emma. Guido thinks they should continue, he sits down on the sofa with something to drink, he'd like to listen. But it goes beyond that, after two songs he's already standing next to Emma and is leafing through the duet book, and Wanda gets the piano part in front of her. During a fast operetta piece, the three of them burst out laughing, during a tender cavatina Wanda hears how the singer supports her mother's voice and lets it shine. A nice man. They want Mozart, the famous duet of Don Giovanni and Zerlina. Wanda takes a brisk tempo but is pulled back by Guido when he starts. She adapts. Behind her back, the two voices start to lead their own life. Together. She hears Zerlina's voice yield, she hears the happy triumph in the final passage and she feels the warmth between the two people behind her while she plays the final phrase uneasily. Sweat beads her neck.

"I'm not staying for dinner. I'd like to catch the seven o'clock train."

"As you wish," says Emma. "Come again soon. But do call, I'm away so often nowadays."

Guido thanks her for playing. He wants to come to her next recital, he admires her, he knows Biermans from the past. Shall he take her to the station?

No, Wanda prefers to walk. She kisses Emma on the cheek. For a moment they stand together in the hall. Wanda is silent.

"You do understand, don't you? I now have a wonderful life. Just like that!"

"Yes," says Wanda. "I'll call. I don't want to intrude."

"You should go to see Frank sometime, I have almost no time for it anymore. The people at the institution like to have family come; actually I did it for them because he doesn't recognize me. Can't you go sometime?"

"I have to go now, otherwise I'll miss the train. And you have to get back to the kitchen."

Wanda feels nothing when she sits in the train, nothing when she gets on the windy platform, when she sticks the key into the front door and climbs the bare staircase. She undresses and crawls into bed without eating. She pulls the blankets over her head.

In her dream she walks through the dark rehearsal area where Tsjak and Gilles are busy with their musicians. Wanda looks for her place which isn't there. The musicians stand arranged in long rows, bent over their drums. In short pants Tsjak is conducting on the stage. Wanda wants to ask the way, she taps a drummer on his shoulder, he turns his head, he's a mongol who looks straight through her. Now Gilles has seen her and starts pointing at her. The drums rumble.

153

Wanda awakens with a pounding head and a raw throat.

Fever. She has to drink. Red face in the mirror. Dull, matted hair. Back to bed and a sudden burst of tears. Then sleep. Coughing. This is not good. She has to call someone. A doctor. Her head is ablaze. It is stuffy. Lie in bed, only lie in bed. The alarm keeps ringing. Or is it the bell? She has to open the door.

"How long have you been lying here?" asks Joyce. She sits with crossed legs on Wanda's bed. Outside air comes from her coat. The violin case stands next to the door. Wanda had crept to the door on her knees. Then everything turned black. Joyce has changed the bed, aired the room and made tea. Wanda had to wash herself with the door ajar so that Joyce would hear if she fell over.

"Give me your key; I'll go shopping for you. Do you have a doctor? No? Then I'll call mine."

Exhausted, Wanda lies in the clean bed. She can only whisper. When she opens her mouth, she has forgotten what she was going to say. Close eyes, sleep.

The doctor is a woman with grey curls. She is not wearing a white coat but a plaid skirt with a sweater. Wanda sighs and coughs at her command. The doctor feels her forehead and looks at the bare legs that lie on the sheet as if paralysed.

"You have a severe pneumonia. I'll give you penicillin, a ten-day course. Bed rest. Drink a lot. Is there someone who can take care of you?"

She is wearing a necklace of matte pearls. Tasteful lipstick, manicured nails. Wanda shivers. Her hair tingles and sticks against her scalp.

Joyce will come by every day, after orchestra rehearsal. And once again in the evening. It's no trouble, she lives nearby.

"I can't go to my mother," says Wanda when the doctor is gone. "She's too busy. And she's always taken care of sick people, she can't stand it anymore. Do you mind?"

"Of course not," says Joyce. "I like to visit you. Now

that you're sick, you talk from time to time. Usually you're so silent."

Wanda lies in bed. In her body the medicines fight the illness. She lets it happen, willingly and without protest. Her skin flakes off, the soles of her feet become smooth like babies' feet and her flesh becomes slack. She sleeps day and night.

"I don't feel like having Biermans anymore. He treats me like a child."

Wanda sits up straight in bed. Joyce has made soup. They eat.

"It always goes like that, towards the end. Then no one feels like having such a long lesson every week. He should let you go your own way a little. Next year you'll be gone."

"I'm going to London," says Wanda. "I want to study with Curzon." She didn't know it. She heard herself say it.

"That nit-picker? That'll be awful, won't it?"

"No. It's just right. I know him from the summer course in Salzburg. He doesn't interfere with anything, he says only what he thinks is wrong. He listens well, Joyce, I can't study at all now!"

"Be glad. When did you last do nothing for a few weeks? Never, right? When you have a vacation, you go and study somewhere else. You can never go a day without."

"And you?"

"I can!" says Joyce. "Certainly since I've been married." She rubs over the red spot on her neck. "I'm happy when I can put that thing in the closet during the summer. I hate always having to pay attention to my hands, always feeling guilty because I don't practise enough, always having to start over. You practise not to deteriorate, it's constantly running to catch up. What a profession."

"It just seems like that. What you practised the previous day you have to practise again, and then you know it faster. You have to take the long view. As if you're building a house with bricks."

And she is letting that house collapse, now that she lies here being sick. Her muscles are forgetting their tricks, her brains are becoming lazy.

"It just doesn't interest me," says Joyce. "I play in the orchestra, sometimes it's nice, I do practise for it, but when I'm off I think it's fine without the violin. Then we go to the movies, or eat, make love, drink wine without pangs of conscience. Can you imagine that?"

"No. I *have* to. I can't be without."

At night she lies awake and flexes her weak fingers. Joyce is happy, she plays music but her real life is elsewhere. With someone else. Wanda can't be together with someone else. She wouldn't know how that's supposed to be. She doesn't understand the others.

When the fever is gone, she's allowed to get up. Eat something at the table, go outside in the afternoon sun. On Joyce's arm she walks in the street, sweating and with trembling legs. She starts sobbing when she's back in bed.

"I can't!"

"Here, blow your nose. You can do everything. You're just tired."

"Lucas. I hadn't figured it out. I never say what I should say. How do you do that, really get to know someone?"

"You have to say what you feel. And the other too. Then it there's nothing to it."

Wanda doesn't even *know* what she feels. Or she feels nothing. At any rate there are no words for it.

"Lucas is not for you," says Joyce. "You should be thankful that you're rid of him. Such a man without a centre who keeps going elsewhere, he has nothing to offer you."

Wanda thinks: my fault. She had nothing to offer him. Does she have a centre? What does she actually mean?

Joyce folds her arms over her stomach and smiles.

"We have to go to the doctor later on. I think I'm pregnant. Finally."

Wanda looks at Joyce's body, at her face. She now notices that the skin under her eyes is puffy, her breasts, arms and cheeks look fuller than before and her eyes shine. The baby is her centre. Or the fact that she can want that baby. So that's why she was finished with the violin. Joyce now has her stomach.

"I'm going to sleep," says Wanda. "You don't have to come this evening. Go and celebrate."

Three times a day at the piano for half an hour. A weak sound. The fingers are still feeble and the back is slumped.

Wanda sweats and plays Bach until everything becomes black before her eyes. It seems as if everything in her head lies open, the partitions between the past and now have sprung a leak and feeling penetrates thinking. The Bach inventions catch her unawares with clear memories: her father sits in the corner of the room on his chair, so real that she can practically hear the newspaper rustle. During another passage she smells the sour odour from Frankie's clothes. The three-part invention in F minor drives her into the street.

The sun stands low, the afternoon is almost gone. Pebbles on the asphalt have shadows like hobnails. The farther she walks, the emptier the streets become. No people to bump into, to avoid, to flee. A swarm of birds rises from the row of trees at the end of the road.

Black dots against a leaden sky. The blood pounds in her head, then it rings in her ears and her skull feels more and more empty. She'd like to be able to place her arms around her big belly, feel the warm hand of a Belgian on her back, Lucas' hip in her side.

*

From the station, Wanda takes the bus to the institution. Between women with full shopping bags she sits still next to the window. She sees villas in a row, then small country houses with big trees, alternating with chunks of meadow. When the houses string together into a village centre, the bus stops and people get off.

"Reehof!" the driver calls out. Wanda sees a shiny white

palace that lies behind a sloping lawn. The entrance roads on both sides of the lawn join under a terrace. Rectangular glass doors close off the building. Behind it is the park.

It looks as though no one is present in the white house. The curtains hang motionless behind the windows. Wanda walks around it. A strangely built man or boy is digging between the trees. He calls out something to her. She doesn't understand it. In the woods she spies a cement bunker: the gatehouse. Wanda taps against the window and is let in. It smells of sourish powdered coffee and old cigarettes. Wanda sits down at a formica table across from the man who invited her in. He is wearing a peculiar outfit, a habit. Wanda thinks the guard is mentally handicapped before realizing that he is a religious.

The man notices her looking and says: "Brothers penitent. For many years we cared for the patients. Now there are doctors and young people who have studied. There are just a few of us left. And old, old."

He puts on thick glasses to look in the patients' book.

"Yes, yes, that's what I thought: Wiericke, Frank – the Otter pavilion. Ward for bed-ridden patients. It's in the back of the property, almost at the edge of the dunes. Still a good walk for you."

The friar takes out a map to show Wanda how she should walk.

"Visiting is actually on Saturdays, did you know that? You must not have been here for a long time."

"Yes," says Wanda. "I'd also like to speak with my brother's doctor, do you think that's possible?"

"He's here, I saw his car. You know what, if you start walking now, I'll call him for you and if he has time he'll come to the ward. Then you'll meet him there."

Slowly she walks through the park, past sloping fields of grass and stately chestnut lanes. The square, modern buildings that stand here and there in the woods have glass façades and are named after small animals. The names are painted on wooden signs next to the entrance doors: Squirrel, Hedgehog, Mole.

A group of boys is raking leaves; on the path stands a wheelbarrow to put them in. Wanda walks by on the other side of the path, timid, pretending to hurry. His red hands filled with autumn leaves, a man walks towards her.

"It has to be done," he says. His teeth stand in a festering bed of shiny gums. Wanda nods. A bald mongol directs his binoculars on her and watches her.

Her heart beats restlessly. Slowly now, look at the signs. There, further on, to the right, there's the Otter, Frankie's house.

The door is locked and there is no bell. Wanda sits down on a low wall next to the entrance. The air is cold and misty. She tastes a dash of salt. The dunes stretch out behind the railway line that borders the grounds. Behind the windows of the Otter a light goes on, it throws a pale path of brightness on the pavement.

Over the path two men with a hand truck filled with food are approaching; a friar and a live-in help, thinks

Wanda. The friar is wearing an orange windbreaker over his robe. He opens the door with a key which hangs on his uniform and looks at Wanda.

"Would you like to come in?"

Wanda gets up and behind the stack of bread and bottles she slips into the entrance hall. The men disappear into the kitchen with their purchases, the door slams closed and Wanda stands in a deserted space. It's stuffy, the air is heavy and sweetish. From all sides hallways lead to this inner square. Weak twilight falls on the grey linoleum through a window in the ceiling, half covered with autumn leaves. Stacked chairs stand against the wall; muffled giggling and clattering of dishes come from the hall into which the men pulled their cart.

At the back of the hall stands a black grand piano with a closed lid.

161

She needs eighteen loud steps to reach the instrument. She pulls her arms out of her sleeves when she sits down. The coat falls back onto the floor. A Bechstein. The music stand is tooled, carved. The paint is flaking and the low, broad pedals are dull-looking. Old ivory on the keys. A low chord, deep echoing strings. Slightly out of tune. A wonderful sparkling treble. Why the Italian Concerto just now? She doesn't know. She plays.

The friar and his helper approach from the kitchen. They remain standing, leaning against the wall. She doesn't see them. Someone sticks a key in the outside door and stamps the leaves from his feet at the entrance. She hears nothing. There is only the movement of the music, the strange space which she explores and fills with familiar sounds. Finally she breathes again.

A shadow across the floor. As quick as lightning a dark figure slides across the light linoleum, with jerking movements. A nurse in a white smock runs after it but stops suddenly at the edge of the dim hall. The young man crawls closer to the piano. Wanda sees him out of the corner of her eye and smiles. Under the piano he pulls his legs up to his chest and remains lying curled up until the music is silent. Then a croaking, wild sound comes from his throat: "Mbwaah, *mbwaah!*"

Wanda bows her head and solemnly starts the slow part. She envelops her brother with the heavy base chords and above it, with her right hand, spins a heavenly song.

Chapter seventeen

H

ow fresh and bright the morning is in Albi!
Bouw put on a new, light cotton shirt with short sleeves.
The car stank of sweat and wine. He opened all the windows
and drove out of the city. As he approached Toulouse he
noticed that he tended to slow down. Why hadn't he passed
that slow truck, what was there to see in those sterile small
parks in the outskirts, why did he brake so forcefully when
the traffic light was only yellow?

Bouw expected the town centre to be busy. Better
stop the car somewhere and look at the map carefully.
Maybe while sitting on a terrace. It's supposed to be a
beautiful city of pink stone.

He looked at his bare forearms. Grey-blond hairs,
rough skin with coffee-coloured spots here and there. Its

stretch gone, its shine worn off. The stomach bulged heavily over the belt on his trousers, and in the rear-view mirror he caught a glimpse of the thin hair that crept steadily back on his head.

He had a stomach like a board when he met her. From rowing. A thick head of dark blond hair. He didn't think he'd ever lose it. Never slow, never tired, then.

The way to the south was indicated quite clearly. The signs to Foix led him around the centre to a narrow road through industrial zones. He shrugged his shoulders. To Foix.

"There's a lady for you," the friar-guard had said. "A relative of patient Wiericke. She's waiting in the Otter." It was autumn; it was the end of a long day. He had wanted to go home and had quickly walked in to check if anything had come up; he was already holding his car keys.

Frank Wiericke. A child with threefold bad luck. Not only Downs syndrome, but also brain damage because of a difficult birth and subsequent malnutrition during the occupation. Not a sociable, affectionate mongol, a ray of sunshine in the house, playful and thankful like a sweet dog. Frank was a sullen boy who barely let himself be cared for. He didn't speak, recognized no one and let no one approach him. He didn't dare to walk but instead crawled over the floor from the ward to his own spot against the wall where he banged his head. The head of the department had gym mats installed against the walls. When Bouw started work in the Reehof, he found the severely retarded in bed. All day long they lay on rubber sheets between the rails of their beds and were fed and washed on a strict schedule by the friars. He had introduced a semblance of life by fixing up a kind of living-room with mattresses on the floor. The bedridden patients were carried there every morning so that they could look at the trees through the reinforced glass. He directed the nursing staff to play with the patients. He gave them a budget to buy balls and drums. The brothers penitent shook their heads. That's not how it should be. Whoever cannot do anything should lie in bed and be looked after. Order, cleanliness and devotion, that's what it was about. Whoever understands nothing cannot pray; praying must be done for him. Religious services and the attention to cleanliness filled the days, the rest was superfluous. With sorrow, the friars had to watch a gym teacher come to the home to teach the patients how to move. A professional staff was recruited, young people who couldn't mop, who neglected messes in order to sing a song with a patient.

It was a tough long battle which the friars had to lose. They were getting older and weaker and had time against them.

Bouw waged the battle slowly and politely, but unrelentingly. The passive resistance irritated him, the pious selflessness made him furious, but the aspect of the old men in their strange robes also inspired his respect and compassion. A pension plan was created.

And a psychologist came, fresh from the university and steeped in the very newest theories of learning.

Pamiers. The land had become green. No longer any mega-supermarkets, car companies and furniture warehouses. The mountains loomed in the distance. The road started going up. Bouw was approaching the Pyrenees. He wanted it and he didn't want it.

"An approach–avoidance conflict," said the psychologist. "They are afraid of the retarded and want to run away; but they're also fascinated by them and want to get closer. The result is that they remain stuck at a point which is determined by fear and curiosity. That's how you should select your staff. They shouldn't be at too great a distance from the patients, but they shouldn't throw themselves at the patients either, straight through their defences. Then they have no distance and can't reflect."

Through the learning theory the Reehof got another character. The residents were tested, development profiles were made and courses for learning were formulated.

The purpose of such a course was no longer determined by the demands of society or the parents, but by the supposed needs and measured capacities of the retarded themselves.

Bouw grinned. What a time! Even the most profound idiot was given a programme. Make eye contact, extend a hand, make a sound. For hours on end nurses would teach a patient how to take off a sock. If the behaviour went in the right direction, the patient got a treat. Meals became circuses. The residents were allowed to choose what they wanted to eat and had to do as much as possible themselves.

Platters would crash down on the floor, they shoved the food in with both hands and grabbed meatballs from their neighbours' plates.

Above all Bouw had talked. With the nursing staff, to slow down the pace of innovation; with the friars, to soften the feeling that they had done everything wrong; with the families of the residents, to explain why everything had to be done differently. The worst was the dismantling of the living environment: on the orders of the psychologist, paintings and decorations were taken from the walls and the radio was turned off. All those colours, forms and sounds confused the patients so that they no longer knew what they should pay attention to. The space should become poor in stimuli, then the attention of the retarded would naturally be directed to the one red ball rolling towards him. Inhuman, said the friars; cheerless, said the staff, it looks like a laboratory. An absolute necessity, argued the psychologist. Bouw explained patiently how beneficial the quiet was for the easily overloaded stimulus-selection mechanism of most of the residents. He was proved right. Gradually the patients started to understand what they should pay attention to, and the caretakers noticed that the bare surroundings were of assistance to them. It helped everyone except Frank Wiericke.

He stopped in Foix to eat something. He walked on the walls of the square castle and looked at the mountains in the distance. Soon he would be there. What should he do, where would he go?

The years in the care for retarded had trained him in looking, considering and negotiating carefully. He had started
to like the slow process. The development of an imbecile
is so slow, almost unnoticeable, that by comparison a normal
child shoots ahead like a rocket through its own history.
All the workers who felt comfortable at the Reehof knew
the love of slowness and the joy of a minuscule step forward.
It made the world into a safe place, without competition
and without disappointment. It suited Bouw. He could
leave rapid progress to his mother, with her capriciousness
and her unrealistic expectations for his career. By going in
this direction he didn't have to become a surgeon but could
calmly go into an area about which no one knew anything,
a hidden path that led, twisting, to a high policy function
in the Ministry of Health.

When at last he sat behind his desk there, he had to
watch how the changes that he had set in motion in the
care for the retarded had been carried to an extreme. The
retarded were no longer allowed to be called retarded, they
were housed in the city, had to have opinions and had to
protest against discrimination. The institutions were closed.
Nurses became companions, let their hair grow and dis-
dained the tight structure that Bouw found so salutary for
the patients. As inspector he had fought against what he
saw as a quite faulty interpretation of the notion of equality.
In the end the argument was settled by the dwindling flow
of money. The mentally handicapped, as they were now
called, went back into their accommodations in the woods

and there were cared for by attendants with service rosters. There was no more money for experiments. Everyone had lost.

When he saw Wanda for the first time, he was still an incredible coward. Against the brothers penitent he dared, in the institution he was the boss, but if someone got too close to him he didn't know what to do. He politely abandoned girlfriends as soon as they wanted to live together or have children. He had control over his life. It was partly living.

Tarascon. The vegetable crates filled with courgettes and grapes stood almost on the roadway. Honking loudly, a car tore across the narrow bridge. From loudspeakers that were mounted everywhere on houses and lampposts, music sounded at full blast. Past the church was the turn-off to Ax-les-Thermes. There was snow on the mountains and the air felt fresher.

Irritated, he had walked back to the Otter that autumn day. He had put the keys back into his pocket and grumbled at relatives who wanted to speak with him at times that it suited them. Why didn't he let her make an appointment for another day? Maybe he didn't want to go home and hid his loneliness behind an excessive devotion to duty. No, nonsense, he was just curious. Frank was a difficult patient. He knew the mother who came by once a month and always wanted to leave quickly. A nervous woman who wasn't able to be interested in her child. There was something wrong with her, it was never possible to start a real conversation with her; there was something superficial and prickly about her which made all attempts fail. Her visits became less frequent, and Bouw no longer sought her out when she came to the ward.

It seemed to make no difference to Frank. He sat in his corner and banged his head against the padded wall. He screamed, not in pain but to amuse himself. Once a nurse's aide had been able to catch his attention by playing her recorder. Frank stopped moving and turned his head to the sound. He laughed and was quiet. When after a month the young woman stayed away, he fell back into his old habits. Every attempt to entice him with drumming or singing failed. No one in the permanent nursing staff could play the flute.

170   Walking on the path to the entrance he already heard the piano. He opened the door with his service key and wiped his feet. In the kitchen passage brother Theophile and his helper Guus stood looking into the hall, their arms crossed. Bouw squinted and saw more people standing in the half-light. He approached cautiously and followed the gaze of the nurses who were standing against the wall. Frank Wier-icke was lying under the piano. He laughed. He didn't hit himself. He didn't bang his head against the floor. He lay listening contentedly. When it was silent he said something.

Bouw had a lump in his throat and had to blink. It wasn't until then that he looked at the woman behind the grand piano. Her coat trailed from the piano stool. She placed her pale hands against the keyboard and bent sideways from the waist to look at Frank. Then she played again, a slow and sad piece. Amidst all these silent people, in that crazy setting, the woman sat and played for her brother, in the dark.

The festival city of Tarascon with its silly tower lay behind him. He had already plunged into the valley that would lead him to Ax and drove under plane trees with their mottled trunks that stood along the road. After Ussat, the bottom of the valley widened. At his right the river murmured towards him; beyond it rose the mountains, inexorable, inaccessible and steep. That's where he had to go. It was four o'clock in the afternoon.

Chapter eighteen

"Bouw. Bouw-bouw-bouw!"

172

Giggling, Wanda lets herself fall back and pulls the sheets up to her chin.

"How did you get that name? Tell!"

"It's my mother's fault," says Bouw. "She had something going for the Belgian royal family. The abbreviation is mine, from when I started talking. I've just left it like that; you can't in all seriousness be called Boudewijn. Now take a sausage, here is the mustard."

Wanda sits up. They lean against the wall with the pillows in their backs and eat fries from paper bags. When Wanda wants to lick her fingers, Bouw takes hold of her wrist. He takes the fingers in his mouth, one by one, and carefully licks grease and salt from her sturdy hand. With lips and tongue he walks the underside of the wrist with its veins and tendons, the soft skin which leads to the inside of the elbow; he sucks a mark into the bend of the arm, Wanda lifts her hands above her head and his mouth slides to her armpit, he blows and bites and kisses.

"Wanda is a terrible name too. Or am I not allowed to say that?"

"My mother. Everything is light opera for her. It has to sound nice. She liked it, with those two w's. I was always embarrassed by it. I would have preferred being called Laura."

Wanda throws her naked arms around his neck and kisses him with her greasy mouth.

After the visit to Frankie, Bouw had walked with her through the park. She had trembled on her legs. Are you feeling all right, he had asked, you look pale, come in the car, have you eaten at all?

In the restaurant they had sat across from each other and had been surprised at being on a first-name basis so quickly. Bouw had talked about Frankie, about his work at the Reehof and the changes over the last few years. He listened attentively when Wanda spoke about life with her brother at home; he asked how that had been for her, how she felt, what she wanted to do with her life and her talent. I'm talking too much, she had thought, it's the wine, it's the faintness.

He took her home. In front of the door they sat talking in the car until two o'clock in the morning. His relationships, her affairs, as if they felt that the information would hurt too much later. Now it was still possible.

He hardly dared to kiss her good-bye, but Wanda took his face in her hands and kissed him.

It wasn't until an hour later that she stuck the key in the door and dizzily leaned against the doorpost. He had started the car, she waved at him and almost skipping she walked upstairs.

They have cleaned up the leftovers, the big light is off, Bouw drinks a glass of beer and Wanda some water. Bluish light falls through the large windows. High in the sky clouds push past the moon. She has to go home. She wants to stay. She closes her eyes and hears Bouw put his beer glass on the floor. She listens to his breathing. He turns over on his side and Wanda pushes her buttocks against his soft penis. He sighs and puts his arm around her.

When she stayed overnight in Bouw's house for the first time, she didn't see much of the house. At her second visit, a grand piano stood in the living-room.

"I've rented one for you; that way you can suit yourself when I'm not here. You won't have to go to that school to practise. You can get used to things here."

She had blushed. He had given her a key. While Bouw worked at the Reehof, Wanda was practising in his house.

In the evening she played for him what she had practiced that day. They ate in the city or in the small kitchen, went to a movie or to bed. They were sufficient to each other and missed no one.

After Wanda had obtained her soloist diploma with distinction, she started studying to get a stipend for study abroad.

On a Saturday morning she comes panting into the house with a brown envelope in her hand.

"I've got it," she says to Bouw who is still in bed. "I've won. I still have to give a recital to present myself, with the jury there too. But I've got it!"

Bouw is silent. He pulls her into bed with coat, shoes and envelope. He rips the clothes from her body, he presses her arms against the mattress so that she can't move, can't leave. He goes into her without looking at her.

Later they stand in the shower together and he takes her dripping face in his hands.

"If you really want it so much, you should do it," he says. "As long as you come back."

"Good," says Wanda.

"After that recital you should give a party," says Bouw. "You should celebrate such an achievement. What are you planning?"

Nothing, Wanda is planning nothing. She can't think of a party. Who would come, what should she talk about? How should she behave?

"I'd like best to be with you, at night. No other people."

He takes a day off when Wanda has her recital. After the applause and the speeches they go home and Wanda sees that the room has changed. Glasses and bottles are standing on the cleared-off desk and a cloth is lying on the grand piano; on it are plates and platters with food. Oblong copper pans are kept warm by blue flames. It's summer, the garden doors are open to the terrace where Bouw has placed chairs and benches. Wanda puts the flowers she received in vases and buckets.

The guests arrive; together Wanda and Bouw stand in the doorway and welcome Biermans, Emma and Guido, fellow students and contemporaries, even Lucas, even Tsjak. On the terrace Joyce with her enormous stomach sits on a high chair. Gonnie has come with Peter, who shyly introduces his new wife to Wanda. Later in the evening the Heidelbergs walk in. People from long ago. What do they want from her? Wanda shivers. Sweet of Bouw to have taken such trouble. She sees him talking with Emma, he fills Guido's glass, Biermans is standing there too. The four of them look at Wanda, they raise their glasses and toast her.

"Come and sit down for a moment," says Joyce. "That doctor of yours is a sweetheart. Are you happy?"

Wanda reflects. People come, you speak with them and make music with them, you make love with them, and suddenly they're no longer there and there are other people with whom you talk and make love.

"I didn't believe that such a party would be nice. Bouw did get his way. Is that good?"

"Yes, that's very good. Enjoy it. Feel here, it's moving!"

Joyce guides Wanda's hand to her taut stomach. Something pushes from within against the stomach wall, a little foot, an elbow! With a start, Wanda pulls back her hand.

"You played magnificently!" says Guido. "During the Beethoven variations I had tears in my eyes, so pure and simple the way you did that. My compliments, my thanks!"

Wanda slips away, to the kitchen where Emma is putting smoked salmon on platters. She has to ask it, she has to say it right, otherwise Emma won't get it. Is she thinking of Mr De Leon because she played? Or because she's with Bouw? What did she actually want to say?

"Mum, do you have that too? I was thinking about the past."

"Oh sweetheart, please open the faucet for me, I've got such fishy hands. Thank you!"

Emma washes her hands and looks at her daughter.

"On a day like today you shouldn't think about the past. You always worry so! Just look at what your life is like now, with such a marvellous career and such a sweet friend. Forget about the past, dear, I do that too."

Lucas comes into the kitchen and snatches some salmon from the platter.

"If you're invited by an orchestra in London, just tell them that you're bringing your own conductor, right? You're a lucky dog to have won that grant! When are you going?"

She should be happy. She is happy about how she played. She has won a prize, received a scholarship. And yet.

"I start in September. I'm also going to do chamber music. And three recitals, that's already set."

Or should she stay here, with Bouw? Joyce says yes, Biermans says no. Don't think about it now. Everything will turn out the way it will, she can't do anything about it.

In the garden the roses and the just-mowed lawn are fragrant. Bouw gives her another glass of cool wine and says that the party was a success. And yet, she thinks, and yet.

Letters arrive from London. Mr Curzon expects her at the end of August. An apartment with a piano and a kitchen has been reserved for her in a house that belongs to the university. She is supposed to form a trio with the other prize winners, a Swiss cellist and a violinist from Spain. She places her signature under the contract.

"I'm going to visit you," says Bouw. "For sure once a month. And you'll come here. We won't lose each other."

Wanda has no doubts as long as she sits at the piano. Practice. Work all day, undisturbed, on her technique. Discover new pieces, hear other ideas, hold your own with better musicians. When Bouw comes home in the evening, her face is red from exertion and excitement. She talks about her plans and already seems to be living partially in the new city.

Bouw is silent. After dinner they visit Joyce. Wanda has bought a bear which they are bringing to the baby. Joyce is lying on the couch with her daughter in her arms.

The baby has alabaster eyelids, it has just finished drinking and is sleeping peacefully. The small lips make little sounds of satisfaction. Wanda doesn't touch the baby, she doesn't want her on her lap. The child belongs to Joyce. She has lost her friend.

"I think that's so wonderful", says Bouw on the way back in the car. "A mother with a baby. See how Joyce is totally absorbed in it? Do you ever long for that?" Wanda shakes her head no.

She packs two suitcases, one with clothes and one with music. In a week it'll be that time. Bouw is tired and easily irritated. He doesn't understand that Wanda doesn't want to say good-bye to her mother. He wants to organize a dinner party, but Wanda has no time.

"She's going to miss you just like you'll miss her," he explains.

"But I won't miss her at all," says Wanda. "When I'm there I won't miss anyone. I'll play."

Unsmiling, Bouw walks to the open suitcase.

"That's just it! You miss no one! Most people make an effort, they take along photos and cherished things. In your suitcase there's nothing but work. Not the books you got from me. Nothing of ours to have with you over there. You simply can't."

Wanda is shocked by his outburst. At night she tries to console him. She doesn't understand him. He sighs in her hair.

"I don't know what it is. I can't imagine that things

179

will break down between us, and yet I'm worried. Maybe I'm jealous of you. Of the fact that you can still study for a while without tying yourself down. No, that's not it. I'd like to be your piano."

"But I play on any and all pianos," says Wanda. "Bechstein, Bösendorfer, Steinway, the most atrocious grand pianos or the most beautiful ones. I sit at them and I play."

The store fronts in London are painted in a dark green colour that is almost black. On them the names of the owners are written in gold. Wanda lives very near the British Museum which is free for everyone and where it is never crowded in the extensive halls and rooms. There is a manuscript department. A string quartet by Mozart lies in the display case. *His* hand has moved over that rectangular sheet, he drew the notes between the narrow staffs, *he* thought up the theme that is still played everywhere today.

There are three apartments in the house. Wanda lives downstairs; her piano stands in a room built out into the garden. It is cold. Above her lives the cellist from Switzerland. The violinist is lodged in the attic. Without having to adjust she falls into life in London. She studies new pieces and old pieces once again. Her teacher, a proper, portly gentleman with wet combed hair, helps her to make contact with an agency. From her next visit to Holland she brings back her concert dress.

With the Swiss cellist she practises a Beethoven programme. They understand each other without having to say much. He speaks poor English and Wanda barely any

German. No connection is as close as that between the cello and the piano because the heart of the pitch for both instruments lies in the same range. They have to draw back for each other, otherwise one is drowned by the other; when they join, the sound is so intense that it continues vibrating in the bodies of the players. He is a boy with a head of curls, from a large family. Laughing he sits in Wanda's back room with his wide instrument between his knees. Playing makes them warm, and the beautiful melody lines that run so intimately through each other make them excited and overconfident. With cello and bow in his left hand he bends over the keyboard to look at the piano part. His right hand touches Wanda's shoulder. Warmth radiates from his body to her face.

Bouw comes; they stay in a hotel for a weekend because Wanda's bed is too narrow. He doesn't belong in a student house. When he picks her up, he shakes the cellist's hand in the hall and is immediately bothered by the violin sounds from upstairs. Rubbing his hands he paces up and down Wanda's chilly rooms. He wants out.

    Wanda thinks of the rehearsals with the Swiss and also decides it's better to keep things separated. Pressed close to Bouw she walks along the river. They take a taxi to Kenwood House to see Rembrandt's self-portrait. They sit a whole afternoon across from each other in a quiet café. She knows once again: this is how it should be, she belongs with this man. How can she then have done it with Thomas? She walked up the stairs behind him. He carried the cello high in front of him. How did she end up in that narrow boys' bed, and why? Don't think about it, it didn't happen if she doesn't think about it. It happens because of the playing. You feel every muscle, all of your body, all day you're conscious of your arms, buttocks, stomach. And he too. Don't think about it anymore. It's nothing.

They sail in the boat to Greenwich. The sun comes through the November clouds and shines on the warehouses, the palaces and the turbulent water. The white buildings lie perfectly arranged at the foot of the hill. They wander through the former hospital, climb to the Observatory and look at Cook's maps in the museum. It's an afternoon without creases or folds; it is as it should be.

On the way back they stand in the wind on deck.

"I'm thirty," says Bouw. "I begrudge you nothing, but this isn't right. Can't you come back after Christmas?"

His eyes tear in the wind. He is a tourist who has no business being here.

"I want to buy a house, I want to marry you. I'd like to have you with me."

Wanda nods.

Still, it takes until early spring before she packs both her suitcases again and leaves. In the new house Bouw has furnished a large room for her. All the music lies on shelves along the wall and in the middle of the living-room stands the grand piano, the welcome home present, the wedding present, the offering.

It's not as easy to get concerts here, but thanks to her London management, Wanda gets a start and plays regularly. She takes care of her English obligations by travelling back and forth quickly by airplane.

Wanda exhales deeply. She's home.

Chapter nineteen

While she slept, the illness slowly crept back into her bones. The curative influence of the sulphur had worn off, and fluid started collecting in the joints between periosteum and connective tissue. The body wanted to turn and bent a knee, then tried to let an elbow change position. Pain shot up and pricked through the sleep. It was four o'clock in the morning and Wanda woke up with stiff limbs.

Rheumatism was the rope which tied her to this yard. Like a goat she stood on her piece of property and the rope determined how far she could walk. Awful? Not at all. She had walked, run and jumped enough. After her marriage she had become a fugitive.

She placed the painful hands on her stomach under her nightshirt and carefully stretched her legs. By now the mountains were slightly darker than the air above them. Soon the sun would come. She would take a bath, put on clothes that lay in their fixed place in the closet, she would sit down on the balcony in the chair where she always sat.

Never more live out of a suitcase which often hadn't even arrived with the airplane. She had always carried the music with her in a shoulder bag, but now and again she'd had to borrow or hurriedly buy dress, shoes and toothbrush in a strange city. The suitcase had never been heavy. Lifting is the worst thing for your hands; they bend around the handle, the weight pulls at the muscles so that they become worn out and don't want to move anymore.

Things that don't work. A key which doesn't fit in the hotel room door for which it was intended. A taxi which cannot squeeze through the traffic. A hall heater which doesn't start. People were all too eager. The greedy impresario, the concert hall manager, the piano tuner – all were happy when Wanda came. The conductor, the journalist, the little girl with the programme on which she wanted a signature. Talk. Everyone wanted to talk. It was as if she had known these people for years. She had a part in a play whose rules she didn't understand. She just did it because everyone did; they must know how it should be done. When she lived like that she didn't mind, she didn't think about it. She lost things: a good pair of manicure scissors, a sweater she was attached to, a book, a shawl. She left the bouquets she received in the hotel. She didn't care, that's how it was supposed to be. Resting she did in other hotels or in rented houses in which she became restless again after two weeks. She didn't know the streets in the cities where she was, and she had no idea of the money in her wallet. After the concert she drank wine at a table set for them, everyone was laughing, she and the conductor got something to eat, he took her hand under the tablecloth as if he were her lover. Nothing made sense. She thought of Brahms. She'd have a fight in order to be able to play in the hall for a few hours in the morning, she sucked up to the piano tuner just to get her way and she put up with everyone's chatter. She concentrated on the concert and forgot her umbrella, her gloves and her mascara. She lost stacks of mail, presents and souvenirs. Now she even regretted it when she broke a favourite plate.

She smiled to herself and stood up. Like a dangerous animal, the grand piano was locked up in the room. Wanda circled around the instrument, softly and carefully, as if trying not to attract attention. It was still cool on the balcony and silver drops lay on the leaves of the sage plant. She leaned her arms on the wall and looked at the mountains. Why shouldn't she sit at the piano this morning and see how it feels, she thought. Or was that no longer possible now that she was thinking all day long? Formerly she never thought, at any rate not in words, like the others. She had sounds in her head. By always thinking in notes she managed to preserve the structure of fugues, sonatas, nocturnes and études. That was her home and that's what she took care of. Her music thoughts were at odds with the fabric of words made by the others. Only on the piano did she express herself. Her only hope in reaching someone lay in those sounds. It used to.

Through the hall window Wanda looked out over the village. The door of the hotel stood open and lights were on in the kitchen. She took her walking stick and strode down the road. In the hotel it smelled of coffee. Françoise, the owner, stood in the kitchen doorway with baguettes under her arm. She wore a blue-checked apron and started talking as soon as Wanda came in. While talking she brought bread, butter and blackberry jam. She poured coffee and sat down across from Wanda.

The way in which Wanda repeated sonatas in her head was the way in which Françoise told stories. Over and again her mother died after a life of poverty and hard work. Every time again her father brought fugitives across the border in secret at night, along a road that only he knew: small children, women wearing thin-soled dancing shoes, starved and frightened. Over and again her father was silent when he came home, and in every story traitors shot him down. Together Wanda and Françoise sang the same refrain every time: war destroyed men and tore the soul from women's bodies.

The postman came in and sat at the table with the women. In the black leather bag he looked for the stack of bills for the hotel. Sighing and complaining, Françoise poured him coffee.

"May I give you your mail now too, madam? That'll save me a walk up."

A bill from the piano company in Toulouse. A newspaper from Holland. A letter with vaguely familiar handwriting:

> *In connection with my work I'm going to be in the Pyrenees this coming week. If you think it's a good idea, I'd like to see you. Think about it, I'll be in touch with you.*
> *Bouw.*

Chapter twenty

At a quarter to seven the alarm on Bouw's side of
the bed goes off. He groans and turns over, pushes close
against Wanda, against her soft, sweet-smelling body.

"You have to get out, you have to go to work," she
whispers into his neck. She pulls up her legs and tries to
push him out of bed.

"Just a little longer," says Bouw. "I won't see you
again until this evening."

The wrestling becomes an embrace. They make love.
Then he jumps up, pulls open the curtains and strides to
the bathroom.

Wanda crawls under the blankets where it smells of
sweat and semen. Bouw sings in the shower. Naked he
comes into the room. Wanda watches him through her

eyelashes – Schumann's Toccata. Strong, compact, bursting with vigour. His seed sticks between her thighs. He goes off, to Frankie and the friars. When she bends over this afternoon, she'll suddenly feel him flow out of her. And this evening she'll hear his car coming. The engine will turn off, the car door will slam shut, and then he'll stand in the kitchen. He always comes back.

The shirt he wore yesterday is still lying on the floor and Wanda puts it on. She wants to have his bitter smell against her body all day long; the shirt is soft and supple when it has been worn by Bouw for a day. It feels cool against her nipples and is as long as a dress. She puts her fingers in her curls and rubs her scalp. Music comes from the kitchen. Lifting her legs high she dances towards it.

Bouw's hair has been combed flat over his head. His face shines and he is smoothly shaven. He has toasted a slice of bread for Wanda and has spread it with butter and honey. His bag stands next to the door. Wanda brings the coffee to her mouth, the smell unexpectedly hits her as strange, and she suppresses a gagging motion. She can't get a bite of the toast into her mouth. The golden butter melts slowly on the bread. The hands of the kitchen clock crawl from stripe to stripe. Soon he'll get up, will put on his coat, will leave. An enormous fatigue makes all her muscles weak, she hangs on her chair, she can barely stay upright. Go now, just go now.

When he comes home in the evening, Wanda sits freshly washed at her piano, in jeans, her bare feet on the pedals.

"Surprise!! After your concert I'm taking a vacation. We're going to catch up on our honeymoon, Mrs Kraggenburg! Just continue playing, I'm going to cook something Italian, that'll take a while."

He leaves the door open. Wanda looks for Scarlatti, to maintain the mood.

Bouw pulls a travel guide from the bookcase and reads to her. Orvieto, San Gimignano, Siena.

The lamp light shines on his hair. They are married. He was angry that she didn't want a wedding, but he didn't force anything on her. When they came out of the city hall, they drove to the sea. All day they walked. There was a salty wind that blew foam across the sand. They ate out in the restaurant at the port; afterwards they slept in their own bed.

"Can't you get away for ten days or so? Or does that make you restless, is it too long?"

"Perfect," says Wanda. "I think I'll be able to do without a piano for two weeks. With you. Then I'll start on the programme for America. Plenty of time. You planned it exactly right."

Bouw's expression hardens. He lets the book drop into his lap and looks at her. "Do you really want to make that tour? Two *months*, that's awfully long."

"I have to," says Wanda. "If they ask you something like that you simply have to do it."

"If it goes well there it'll only get worse, then you
have to go again next year."

Wanda nods. It's beyond them. She has to play, she
has to play everywhere, she has to let people hear how it
sounds, what she has in her head. It's the only thing she
can do, the only thing she knows for sure. She has to.

"Dear, how lovely for you, what a wonderful invitation.
Such an honour!"

Emma is radiant. She's become fat, thinks Wanda, fat
and cheerful. Very different from how she used to be. That's
because of the singing, because of Guido, because of her
new life. This is my mother. She's proud of me.

"But first a trip to Italy," says Guido in his deep bass
voice. "You can eat splendidly there. Don't go only to
museums!"

They sit around the kitchen table in Emma's house.
Guido has tied on an enormous apron and walks back and
forth from the stove to the table. He has roasted pheasants
which he serves on a bed of sauerkraut. A new roasting pan,
Wanda notices. And new dishes and other kitchen chairs.
The countertop is the same as before. Her mother's friend
moves in the kitchen as if he belongs there. He doesn't
have to look for tools and cleans up while he's cooking.

After dinner Emma and Wanda do the dishes. Bouw
has retired to the living-room with Guido to have another
drink. What are they talking about? Cars? Women? Women
who go on tour?

There are small pillows of fat on Emma's fingers. With

difficulty she pushes the rings from her fingers and puts them in the soap dish. The thin gold band from Egbert isn't there.

"It became too tight," says Emma while she ties on Guido's apron. Her face is red when she looks up again. With her hands in the soapy water she suddenly starts talking.

"The suds maker, do you still remember? A piece of greyish soap in it, and then beat until the water became splotchy. I always thought that it stank. So many awful things have happened in this kitchen. Fortunately it's behind us; I'm happy about that every day. Your father was a difficult man. And there was good reason for that. The war. A mentally disturbed child. Bouw is good for you, you can just do your work, he accepts it. I stopped singing when Frank was born."

The dishes, the silver. Emma looks at her busy hands. She sure is talking, thinks Wanda. Usually she doesn't say so much, and certainly not about how it used to be.

"Are you sorry that you had children?"

Wanda is shocked by her own question. She dries the glasses carefully. She turns her back to the countertop in order to put them on the table.

"It simply was like that," says Emma. "Afterwards you can think all sorts of things, but it went the way it did. It wasn't easy, that's for sure. And because of the war everything became terrible. Your father was impossible, he had such ideas, he was afraid. I wasn't allowed to leave the house. It was cold. For me the worst was that everything was so filthy, that was even worse than the hunger. You had the piano, thank God you could get Frank quiet. If you ask me honestly: it was hell."

"And when you were pregnant, Mum?"

Emma is silent. She polishes the inside of the roasting pan fiercely with a scouring pad.

"He let it get burned so, I simply can't get it clean!"

"Mum?"

"Oh my dear, I don't remember it anymore. Those years were hard for everyone. We should let it rest."

The dishwater swirls away. Shreds of pheasant and strings of cabbage remain behind on the tiles. Soap bubbles and ridges of grease. Emma dumps the scraps into the garbage can and scrubs the sink with the dish brush until the tiles shine.

*

Siena's large plaza lies in the sun like a warm red shell. They sit on the edge of the fountain; Bouw reads his travel guide and Wanda looks with slightly narrowed eyes at the houses all around. She stretches her legs in front of her, she has taken off her sandals and wriggles her toes. Remain seated here forever, in this hand palm made of stone, in this light.

"There, across the street, that's where we're going," says Bouw.

Hand in hand they stroll to the palace that lies at the bottom of the sloping plaza.

They have to join a group of tourists; a beautifully

made-up woman carrying a stack of papers talks to them in a strange kind of English. She leads the group through a passage to a large hall with painted walls and meanwhile she talks, rapidly rattling, about the history of the palace. Bouw has broken away from the group and walks along the walls, studying his guide. Wanda takes a few steps back. If only that woman would shut up. Wanda isn't interested at all in what she's explaining. It is pleasantly cool in the stone space. She looks up and sees the fresco with a man, a knight on a horse riding through the night, from one city to another. He's wearing a wide cloak; he looks sad and resolute. The rattling woman wants to go on, the group disappears through a doorway and Bouw motions her to come along. Wanda shakes her head and sits down on the bench across from the wall-painting.

He has other things on his mind, that knight, important things. He can't remain comfortably in the safely walled city. Maybe people tried to change his mind. Do stay, finish eating this delicious food, listen to us – but he looks straight through them, it's as though he doesn't hear them. He has to go, alone with his horse through the cobalt-blue night, and no one can hold him back. And yet? If the journey lasts longer and longer, if the city in the distance cannot come closer, would he then not lose his determination? The stars shine with a chill, silvery glow, and it is cold. Someone might be able to bring the knight and his horse to a halt by singing. Maybe he would then do an about-face and ride back to look for the person who sang so irresistibly.

Sick to her stomach. She shouldn't have eaten that

cake. Just close her eyes, be very still, stop the thoughts. Place a hand against the cold marble, and then against the forehead.

After an eternity, a day, fifteen minutes, Bouw comes walking towards her. Wanda looks up surprised, as if she had no longer expected him. Without even a parting look at the knight, they walk back onto the plaza together.

*

Wanda is not rested from the Italian trip. When she starts her exercises in the morning, she is sometimes so tired that she can barely bring her arms to the keyboard. She lies down for a moment and then wakes up when the sun is setting. Sleep pulls at her like a strong stream, all day long. In the bathroom she splashes cold water on her face, over her wrists, in her neck. She sees herself in the mirror: deep-set eyes and dull hair. She shakes her head to throw off the veil of lethargy, she forces herself to walk through the house stamping hard in the hope of finding back her old sturdy self with the fiery eyes. Before she knows it, she's back asleep on the sofa.

Vitamin deficiency, says Bouw. He presses oranges for her and brings home supplement tablets from the institute's pharmacy. Mrs Kraggenburg, three times a day, it says. Large pills with a straw-like smell.

"Actually, I'd rather not be called that," says Wanda.

Bouw looks annoyed.

"What nonsense. Of *course*, that's your name. Why should you keep your father's name? You didn't care for him that much. You're married to *me* now, everyone may know that."

Brusquely he hands her a glass of water.

Wanda swallows the pills.

Images of Egbert dash through her head, she sees him sitting on the floor with Frank, he reaches for a red ball. She should play for Frank again, she thinks, it's been so long. But she's so tired.

"Much better if you'd just cancel."

Suddenly she hears Bouw again. He's talking about the tour. He doesn't want it.

"You just keep going. Two weeks vacation aren't enough. You should really rest up. Your body is protesting, don't you notice? I think that concert tour is too long and too tiring for you."

"But it's *months* from now," says Wanda. "*Months!*"

Bouw sits up with a start. He looks at Wanda intently. Then he jumps up and screams: "Jesus! Months? Wanda! You're pregnant!"

So that's it. *That's* why she sleeps all day long. *That's* why her attention, which she could always direct effortlessly to music, is irresistibly sucked towards her body. *That's* why.

Wanda knows immediately that it's true. But still.

"Me? Pregnant? That *can't* be."

She puts her hands on her swollen breasts, on her stomach.

Her overwhelming urge to sleep has disappeared. Every morning she gets up at the same time as Bouw and eats three slices of bread. She's hungry all day long. She flings the contents of the clothes closets on the floor and puts everything away again, in orderly stacks. She bikes to Joyce. She studies Beethoven's first concerto and Mozart's concerto in A major. Her feeling of happiness bubbles over in the music and results in fast tempos and cheerful interpretations.

"Of course you've called it off by now," says Bouw. "You can hardly travel through America with such a belly. As a matter of fact, I've made an appointment for you with Van Beek. An excellent gynaecologist, and a nice man. He'll take good care of you,"

A gynaecologist, Wanda is startled, thinks of the impossible examination position, backwards on the examining table, the buttocks pushed forward as far as possible, the back of the knees against the cold steel of the leg supports, legs far apart, making room for the doctor who sticks his plastic hand inside, who takes a shiny apparatus with which he will open her wide to be able to peer deep into her.

Doctor Van Beek wears glasses that magnify his eyes. He looks at her affably and asks her how she's feeling and if she's happy with the baby. She doesn't have to spread her legs, he wants to leave the baby in peace, he says. His warm hands press briefly on her stomach and he nods, satisfied. Wanda has to be weighed and then may get dressed again. In his garden a rolling lawn ends in water where a large willow grows.

Van Beek asks how old Emma was when Frank was

born. He scribbles something on a card and makes an appointment for a month from then.

"You may do everything you feel like doing, you're a healthy young mother. Regards to your husband; till next time!"

He takes her hand and places the other one on her shoulder. Wanda dances out through the hall.

The mail brings a letter from the Dutch String Orchestra. It contains a tentative rehearsal timetable and a travel schedule. Rehearsals start a week before departure. There are two programmes. She will play Beethoven and Mozart under conductor Samuel Silberman. In exactly a month she will travel to the rehearsal with her music bag, confer about tempo with Silberman, meet the concertmaster. She has taken no notice of it, she knows it but she doesn't. She lets the letter lie on her desk and sits down at the piano.

199

On Saturday afternoon they walk through the dunes, they run down through the loose sand and slide onto the beach. They fall and remain lying down, close against each other. Then Bouw carries her to the water and together they walk slowly over the hard sand. He has thrown his arm tightly around her, the stitches in her side diminish and disappear. He stands still and kisses her. At night in bed they think up names for the child, they imagine its appearance, hair colour, body shapes. They dream up a character, a life. A daughter, thinks Wanda. She'll look like Bouw and will drink from my breasts.

On Sunday morning Bouw goes to visit his mother. Wanda wants to practise. She doesn't feel at ease in the large house in the Hague and can't keep up with the old lady's conversation. Bouw doesn't force her. He strokes her hair and leaves her alone.

While she is playing it seems as though her stomach is asking for attention. A nagging pain like she used to have when she was going to have her period. On the toilet she sees a blood spot in her panty. That can't be. Should we not have made love so intensely yesterday? Better go to bed. A hot water bottle. Place it against the stomach. Pull up the knees. Far down under the blankets.

When Wanda wakes up it's already dark. She steps carefully out of bed and feels dizzy. Her back hurts and her groins too. She has to hold on to a chair in order not to fall. In the wardrobe mirror she sees her face: greyish white. Thin and bony, her shoulders stick up. The light in the hall is off, in the half-light she walks downstairs. In the living room Bouw sits at the table, looking at a stack of papers. He looks up when she enters.

"What's this?" asks Bouw. He points to a paper. He remains sitting at the table.

"Haven't you cancelled that tour? Didn't we decide that a long time ago?"

The travel schedule. He found the papers of the orchestra. Wanda throws her arms across her stomach.

"How do you actually imagine doing that?"

Bouw asks it in a tone which makes answering impossible. "Shouldn't you discuss this sort of thing first with me? Does Van Beek know about it?"

He lifts the travel schedule between index finger and thumb. Then he lets it go and the papers flutter to the floor.

"I didn't know," says Wanda. She clears her throat; it's as if the words don't want to come out.

"It's pretty clearly indicated here. What do you mean you didn't know? You've been preparing your programme for weeks. You knew it very well. You were going to call off this whole circus, months ago!"

"I forgot."

"Damn. Wanda. That's impossible. You *know* what you're doing. Tear through America in a bus for two months. Tension. Not enough sleep. Bad food. Five, six months pregnant. Think about it!!"

Bouw's face has flushed red. His lips tremble. He remains seated. The large table extends between Wanda and him; the lamplight shines like water on the polished wood.

"But I want to play. I agreed to do it. I have to do it."

Wanda hears herself speak. Her ears are ringing. She tries to hold her back straight. Stabs of pain travel from her back to her legs. She sets her feet solidly on the floor.

"Don't go away," says Bouw. "I had so looked forward to you being at home. With your fat belly. So that we would arrange everything for the baby. Together. You mustn't go. Call them tomorrow. Have them take someone else. You can break your contract for medical reasons. Wanda?"

Wanda lets go of the door. She takes two steps into the room.

Against the inside of her thigh crawls something warm, something wet. She looks down. On the light wooden floor lies blood. Blood drips out of her and splashes against the floor in round spots with offshoots like small hairs. More and more. The ringing in her ears increases, it sings throughout her head. Even though her eyes are open, she sees nothing but black, black with intermittent flashes of light. She hears Bouw's chair legs scrape over the floor. He shouts something. She falls.

Part 3

Chapter twenty-one

Abruptly Bouw's car swerved into a parking lot
and with squealing brakes rammed the high curb. Drive
two thousand kilometres to feel the same sun sting your
eyes. Wallet, sunglasses. He kicked the car door shut with
his heel. He looked over the embankment into the river
bed where filthy water ran lazily between the stones, lapped
against plastic bottles and heaps of garbage. A sweet smell
of rot arose from the stream. Bouw turned on his heels.
Exhaust gases. Car horns. Heat.

Among sweating tourists in shorts, he walked to the
centre. Out of irritation he took steps that were too big so
that he had to zigzag around strollers, bumped into
oncoming people and tripped over the leash on which a
haughty-looking woman was holding her poodle.

What a rotten town, what a bloody noise, what a wretched climate. What an idea to drive here, find a hotel, stay a few days.

Leave again right away, he thought, back to the car, get in, turn around. But his legs walked on to a small square where he saw solid rows of people sit with their feet in a square pond. Nauseated he looked away and at the other side of the road he saw the enormous casino decorated with orange and bright green plastic flags. Boys and girls with naked stomachs and dirty hair sat on the stairs. They leaned against their backpacks and ate from small paper bags. Loudspeakers hung all over the façade and from them disgusting French pop music sounded full blast. In the middle of the traffic circle, lost among buses and trucks, stood the church.

A woman came suddenly from the portal into the road, a car honked and braked with shrieking tyres. An argument, strident voices, a surprising laugh. The church walls were made of concrete; what was still left of old stones was unrecognisably smoothed away behind layers of filler and cement.

Behind the church a road sloped up between white house fronts and plane trees. Bouw moved with difficulty over the uneven cobblestones. He stopped before every shop window to look absently at the displayed wares. Toasters, trusses, roasters. At the end of the street stood a hotel built against an overgrown rock wall. Stairs led to a terrace where people sat drinking under yellow canopies. The tables stood widely separated. Clatter of cutlery came from the open doors. Bouw walked in and reserved a room in the back.

The room was cool, dark and stuffy. Woods bordered right against the back of the hotel. He opened the window and had to use force to push a sizable branch out of the way. Branches popped through the window, redoubled in the mirror on the wardrobe and began to fill the room with the smell of pine. Bouw let himself fall back on the bed and closed his eyes. Mistake. Shouldn't have done it. What now? Call Wanda and tell her that he was here? He imagined a ringing telephone, her voice which would suddenly be forced into his ear, his hesitation because he didn't know what she looked like now. Better not. Better stand unannounced at her door? You couldn't do that after decades of silence, and she hadn't been able to reach him to say whether she would like a meeting or not. He had gone about it the wrong way. What did he actually want?

He loosened his belt and spread his arms wide on the mattress. On the long pillow he moved his head back and forth, as if he wanted to wipe the three-day long drone of the engine from his ears.

It seemed as if he and Wanda were in an elastic web that he stretched with difficulty every day when he went to the Reehof. An elastic that was stretched to the limit when she was on a ten-day tour of England and that sprung back violently at the moment that he picked her up from the airport. They were numbed by the blow then. Why? He had never again felt so connected with anyone else. He wouldn't dream of it. She had swept him along in a form of animal closeness that he never dared again, not even with his own children. Yet he could talk better with Johanna, yet he'd been a nice and involved father, yet he was happy in his family in a calm way.

When Wanda was pregnant he felt like a world conqueror. He had penetrated everywhere, boundlessly, and everything was his. Confusion had always been part of it. When she turned away from him and was busy with her playing, he was overcome with anger, and at the same time the awareness of her undisturbed solitude at the piano gave him peace. Paralysed he had sat behind the door of her practice room, petrified and powerless to go any way at all. When he sat in the audience during a recital, he curled his toes with shame about the way she confided in the public through her playing; in the accents she placed, the tempo fluctuations she introduced, he recognized the sounds she made when she came. He was beside himself with embarrassment but glowed with pride and became weak with emotion.

The parting had been as if you pulled a suction cup from a sheet of glass with which it had formed a vacuum. Bouw grinned at the prosaic image. The right image. He had managed a supreme effort in pulling himself loose. There was danger. The glass could break, the rubber might tear. Irreparable.

He woke up, shot up straight and bumped against the cupboard with the mirror in which the tree branches gently waved back and forth in the dark. Next to the door he found a light switch that didn't work. Groping his way to the bathroom, arms wide, feet shuffling. A yellowish light above the wash basin. His own face with folds and bags under the eyes. Water. The glass fell clinking to the floor but was not broken. Calm, he thought, calm. Get the car. Walk outside a bit. Then sleep. Tomorrow consider what he was going to do. Right now, nothing.

On the terrace, hotel guests were still lingering at their tables. Two couples. An old man with a little girl. Bouw walked down the steps and was on the street. The evening air caressed his skin. It was quiet. He walked into town under the plane trees. A shopkeeper was closing his shutters, a woman dragged a chair inside and closed the door. At a tent in the casino garden men were drinking wine, sitting on plastic chairs. On the square the water was steaming in the empty infirmary basin. He turned into a narrow street behind the hospital and got lost in the steep alleys. The slightly convex streets had wide grooves on both sides, interrupted here and there by small drains in which water swirled away, hissing and spluttering. Bouw stopped at an intersection of alleys: everywhere smoke plumes, spurting water and the all-penetrating smell of sulphur. He bent down to put his hand in a gully and pulled it back swiftly. Hot. A quiet town filled with boiling water. He passed by a garden behind an ornate bathing establishment and saw numerous fountains of scalding sulphur water spouting upwards. The water carried withered leaves, cigarette stubs, paper tissues, plastic bags and chewing gum wrappers to the river. That's where his car stood.

The shower water contained no sulphur but chlorine instead, and the temperature didn't exceed lukewarm. He let it pelt his shoulders, on his eyes, through his hair for a long time. Naked he slid between the sheets. Tomorrow, tomorrow onward.

Chapter twenty-two

The pain rages like a wild animal in her body,
pulls ripping at the interior of her stomach, stabs savagely
in her groins and at unexpected moments suddenly comes
to rest for a minute. Then Wanda opens her eyes while she
remains lying still. Bouw has hung a towel over the lamp.
He has taken off his shoes and walks softly around the bed.
Surely he is no longer angry, thinks Wanda. He strokes
her sweating face and sits down next to her on the
bed.

"Does this bother you?" he asks. Wanda remains silent
and he throws back the blanket so he can put a folded towel
under her hips. The pain returns. Wanda's expression turns
inward. Bouw massages her back, with his large hands he
pushes against the flat, painful place right above her buttocks

while constantly whispering that it's all right, that it will pass, a little longer, a little longer.

Hours pass in the ebb and flow of pain. Bouw has lain down against Wanda; he supports her raised legs and blows in her sweaty neck. In between attacks of pain, Wanda stares at the window. They've forgotten to close the curtains. Black, grey, ashen, pale.

Daybreak comes with the most powerful cramp. Wanda turns onto her back. She feels how it slides out of her, the child, her existence in this house, her right to a normal life. She screams with terror and pain.

Bouw looks between her legs on the towel. Later she hears him busy in the kitchen, the tap runs.

The foetus fits in his hand. Bent, bluish. In the clean jam jar. To the refrigerator.

A new towel to lie on. A bright grey window. Stare. His warm hand on her hip. The hand which held it.

When Bouw has fallen asleep, exhausted, Wanda moves away from him. She puts the hand back by his body. She brings her own hands together in front of her chest. She rubs one finger over the other, the palms of her hands push against each other, arch out, make themselves powerful and broad on the turning wrists. Wanda's hands lie tucked away in the hollow between chin and chest.

Under the hot, pelting shower. Strange that the ice within doesn't melt. Strange that all the music in her head has ceased: she hears only the drumming of water on stone.

Poison is locked in that ice. If it melts within Wanda,

the poison will break out and will infect everything. It's her fault, she cannot prevent it.

The thought floats away as soon as it has appeared.

Bouw sits on a chair near the window. He has thrown his hands in front of his face. His broad shoulders shake. Wanda grabs her clothes and leaves the room.

He asks if she's sitting all right, if it's O.K., if the car shakes too much. He puts his arm around her. He kisses her. No, no, no, thinks Wanda. Her head is perfectly still on her neck. When the car makes a turn, the view changes. Finally she sees the garage doors at Doctor Van Beek's practice.

The doctor looks. He pushes firmly downwards against her stomach. Wanda stares at the white fluorescent light. He brings his head with the glasses into her field of vision.

"You had imagined this differently, hadn't you, my girl? Hard for you two, very hard."

For a moment he places his hand against her cold cheek.

What does he mean by differently? She doesn't understand him clearly. It seems as if there are water bubbles in her ears. She hears everything but she understands nothing.

Slowly she gets dressed again.

Bouw and Van Beek sit talking at the desk. It is a low rumbling sound.

"No, not ordinary mongolism. It's a translocation. We had a fellow who made karyotypes of the older mongols years ago. And of the parents, if they were still alive."

"Then you know who the carrier is?"

"The mother was clean. The father was never available, or the research stopped before it was his turn. I don't know."

"Therefore there's every chance that your wife is the carrier. That means amniocentesis next time."

Carrier, thinks Wanda. Doom in my cells, I knew it.

"We'll try again. When you're recovered."

Bouw's breath is against her ear. What is he talking about? Recovered. Again. Poison.

"We still have a whole life, it'll be all right!"

I've got nothing, thinks Wanda. What's he babbling about? It's not about me.

214   In the morning they breakfast silently in the kitchen. Iron pills. Extra vitamins. Bouw leaves for the Reehof. The doorbell. Wanda remains seated. Again. The ringing echoes in her ears. The bell, thinks Wanda. Joyce's face appears in the window. She waves. She points with her hand to the kitchen door. The trees in the garden move along in the wind. Joyce makes coffee. She has left her baby at home and doesn't talk about it either. Still, Wanda thinks of nothing else. Everything Joyce says drowns in baby's crying. Joyce's mouth moves. On her sweater are dried milk and slobber spots. Joyce says that it's terrible, that Wanda feels miserable, useless, worthless and superfluous. Yes, yes. Wanda nods. If only she'd leave. Joyce, Joyce, help.

Joyce puts her coat back on. At the front door she

looks deep into Wanda's eyes. She points to the door of the study. "Now you're going to wash your hands and play. And from now on every day. Doesn't matter what. Play."

She kisses Wanda on her cheek and strokes her hands for a second.

Bouw comes home into a dark house. From the study come slow, controlled Mozart runs. In the kitchen half-filled coffee cups are standing on the table. He sits down, still wearing his coat. He shivers.

*

The orchestra stage manager potters about nervously on the podium. He has a stack of parts pressed under his arm. He places music on every stand. He shifts chairs and with his foot pushes the small boards of the cellists into the right position. The grand piano stands shining. The lid is off.

"Mrs Wiericke, welcome! I hadn't expected you yet! Everything is ready, do you want to warm up?"

He takes Wanda's coat, points to the piano stool, and wipes the instrument.

Wanda feels a wave of joy go through her stomach. How will the piano answer her, what will she be able to demand of the strings, where will the possibilities stop?

Runs. Bass lines in chords, octaves. A piece of the slow part, with very flat fingers, a lot of flesh on the ivory. The stool a fraction lower. The pedals. A chromatic scale over the whole keyboard.

The members of the orchestra enter one by one. Open

violin cases lie on first row chairs of the hall. Violinists stand talking in groups and move their bows across pieces of rosin. A bass player drags his enormous instrument up the small steps. The concertmaster shakes Wanda's hand and says that he looks forward to the tour. A violist with a familiar face joins them.

"We've played together," she says, "in The Future, do you still remember? With Lucas Lansingh."

She has a horse's face. Hideous above such a large viola. Wanda has forgotten her name. She wishes they'd start playing.

From the side Samuel Silberman comes up on the stage. Wanda recognizes him from newspaper photographs. He's shorter than she'd thought. Also older. His back perfectly straight, the elderly conductor walks towards her. He holds the white, pointed baton in his left hand. Dark, straight hair, small eyes, measured gestures. No expression is to be seen on the smooth face.

"Today the 488," he says. "Play through all the way, look at the tempi and the balance. Tomorrow Beethoven. Does that suit you?" Wanda nods. Silberman steps onto the platform and turns towards the orchestra. He introduces Wanda and the musicians tap against their stand with their bows, a mouse applause. Silence. The orchestral introduction. After a few measures he taps his baton.

"Ladies and gentlemen. This is *not* a cheerful piece." Again. Wanda breathes deeply. He has understood. Not a cheerful piece. Questioning, the conductor looks at her.

Wanda nods to confirm that the tempo is good. Then she calmly waits until the orchestra concludes the introduction with two thundering chords.

She lets the simple melody blossom and forces the grace notes into the strict discipline of the bass line. Before the surprised ears of the orchestra members, Wanda conjures a desolate landscape of war, defenceless, damaged. Brazenly she lays bare the structure of the concerto.

She plays the second part subdued, with extreme control, almost without emotion. The winds follow her and the string players hold their breath. Almost without interruption, the rondo follows. Not happy, not cheerful. Mercilessly she introduces the imploring accents; the bass line leads tightly to doom. After the final chord, an uneasy silence hangs over the orchestra.

"Break," says Silberman.

Now Wanda and the old man look at each other. His eyes have become dark and expressive. The orchestra members stumble off the podium. Suddenly Wanda feels the draught in her back, her tired muscles, her light head.

Silberman takes her right hand with both his hands.

"You and I don't need to tell each other anything. With your interpretation you have given me sad pleasure. I hadn't expected this. You have touched me. I thank you."

Wanda lies awake next to Bouw. Mozart races through her head. Thought fragments sometimes push the music aside. The way they see her, thinks Wanda. Bouw wants her sad, ready to be saved. Van Beek saw her desire for a big belly.

Silberman feels an affinity with her. When they went to eat something together after the rehearsal, he sprinkled salt on the table cloth between their plates. He smiled. She is a fraud because she doesn't belong to him, she doesn't want a belly and she isn't sad. They allow her to lie. She can only do what Mozart wrote. That she knows for sure. Sunlight on destroyed land. She is going on a trip, she is going to play. She is going away.

Chapter twenty-three

T he letter lay on the kitchen table. A creamy white sheet folded in three. The lowest segment curled up frivol- ously. Blue ink stripes, a message, a name. The mail always comes with requests and orders; it pulls a web of demands over the world and leaves no one in peace. Wanda had thrown the paper on the table and didn't want to sit down. She wanted to go outside, to look at the mountains. Not to be home when the telephone rang. Doesn't the mail sometimes come with presents, with disinterested greetings, with envelopes full of joy? Sometimes people like to hear from someone who was dear to them decades ago. Well? Not her.

Resolutely she went out of the door and walked around the house to the cemetery. Behind the church, an opening in the wall gave entrance to a wild area, a plateau with low growth, cut up by a system of narrow footpaths.

Wanda walked a way and sat down on a rock. She looked at the snow-capped mountaintops on the far side. A light blanket of morning mist still hung in the valley. She saw the grey buildings of Ax in the distance. Maybe he was there, walking around the narrow streets or he had walked up as she had just done. More than thirty years ago he brought her to the airport. Silent, his mouth an angry stripe. She still flowed from the miscarriage. She couldn't think. Let alone say something meaningful. Something had changed irretrievably. It felt like a relief that the marvellous life with him was over. She didn't know how that was possible. Everything was terrible. He watched her when she walked into the departure concourse. She looked around and walked on.

A motorbike crept up the small road to the high village, a man with an orange crash helmet was riding it. Wanda studied his slow speed, saw how he braked for the turns, disappeared under low-hanging crowns of trees and, accompanied by the increasingly loud rattle of the motor, reappeared. At very steep parts of the road, the rider got off and walked next to his vehicle for a while.

Wanda walked back home. The motorbike stood on a stand at her front door when she arrived. The rider freed his hand from an enormous leather mitt in order to greet her. The piano tuner. In the hall he stamped on the floor tiles. He wore a long leather coat. Wanda watched as he loosened his helmet, put the mittens on a chair and slowly started on a row of tough buttons.

Should she take that coat? He could just hang it up himself. Reeking of sweat. Much too warmly dressed. Calm down, he'll be upstairs soon.

He wanted to go to the toilet. The case with tools stood lost in the middle of the hall. From behind the lavatory door came a splattering sound. Undecided, Wanda remained standing. Go upstairs? Then back down to get him? Now call to him to come upstairs?

She climbed up the stairs and called the tuner when he appeared. The man followed her sighing. His bald head was wreathed with wisps of blond hair. He stopped in the doorway to the balcony room. His red hands akimbo he looked around. He inspected the bookcase, the view, the furniture and the desk.

"There is the piano," said Wanda, pointing at the immense black grand piano standing right in front them. Annoyed, the tuner looked aside and slowly began unpacking his instruments. In a high, hoarse voice he complained of the disadvantages of his profession. The difficult travel, the neglected pianos, the impossible demands of his clients who then rushed him to boot.

He lifted the music stand onto the floor and removed the lids. Groaning he bent down to the pedals and ran a finger over the steel cables. Wanda sneaked to the kitchen and closed the door.

The letter was still lying on the table. She sat down and waited until the familiar tuning sounds started sounding from the piano room, fourths, fifths, always moving up a half note. Sometimes it was quiet. That's when the piano tuner was undoubtedly poring over the list of numbers lying next to the telephone. Or he was examining her last tax return and was going through the incoming mail of the last few months.

She got up, opened the kitchen door softly and banged it shut. Right away there sounded another fifth.

Perhaps it isn't so awful that people want or expect something from you. That they force their way into your mailbox and your house and your head with their demands and their opinions. It's only awful if you're bothered by it, if you think that you have to be obliging to them, have to answer and have to adjust to their expectations. That's why the piano tuner gets no tea and why Wanda sits reading determinedly until he is finished. The hours pass.

He wanted to let her hear what he had accomplished and played loud arpeggios over the whole keyboard. It sounded sharp, thought Wanda. She didn't want to say anything about it at all. The most important thing was to get him downstairs, into his stiff coat, and back on the street. Gloves, helmet and case with it. Hear the motorbike put-put away. But first she had to listen. She gave short, approving comments and signed the bill. She herself would call for the next tuning. She had to leave the left pedal alone, said the hoarse man, otherwise she'd ruin the felt. She had to keep the curtains closed, rub graphite on the pedal cables, polish the keys with rubbing alcohol, but not the black ones, *never* the black ones. Once a week vacuum the interior. He worked himself to death and the clients undid all his work in no time because of laziness and unwillingness.

Furious, Wanda shifted her weight from one leg to the other. As her irritation increased, the tuner became more long-winded. The telephone interrupted his tirade. Now Wanda would have been happy even with Bouw. It was the piano company from Toulouse which instructed its employee to go immediately to the next customer, the delay now amounted to five hours, and that was too much.

Grumbling, the tuner packed up his belongings. When he finally started his motorbike, the sun was beginning to set.

Wanda opened all the windows across from each other and stood in front of the mirror. Grey, short hair with black strands through it. Nice, dark eyes. Skin like a loose curtain around sturdy bones. They would stand facing each other with worn bodies and changed voices. With years and years of unshared memories. With strange views on each other's shortcomings and faults. He had suffocated and imprisoned her with his love, she would say. She had denied him a child, she had walked out, he would say. It no longer worked, he had controlled her. She was inadequate, she had lacked words.

She shrugged her shoulders and poured a glass of wine. She stretched her legs in front of her and lifted her arms above her head. The doors were closed, the intruder had been chased off and in the room stood a perfectly tuned piano.

Chapter twenty-four

P ale-faced, the orchestra members are waiting for their luggage at the conveyor belt. It's six o'clock in the morning and the fluorescent lamps spread a light without shadows. Behind the glass wall of the arrival concourse family members and friends crowded about. A small girl is pressing the palms of her hands and nose against the glass and with big eyes stares straight ahead. Her father waves and walks towards her with his violin case in his arms; smiling, he comes right up to the glass. The child looks but doesn't react.

Wanda nods instinctively. People, fathers leave and come back, or not. Bewilderment is a suitable answer.

Silberman had stayed behind in New York. After last concert they had sat in the lobby of the hotel wide leather chairs. The concertmaster had become drunk and shared his seat with the violist who hadn't left his side during the entire tour. The winds were drinking beer and remained standing. Silberman sat on the edge of his chair with his knees together and his feet straight on the floor. He drank water and looked at Wanda. She had put her sourish wine on the floor and wanted to tell him that the concerts had been her salvation, that he had taken care of her, played around her protectively and led her like a wise father, that she was grateful. But which words, and how to express them? She was silent.

"Next year in Tel Aviv," Silberman had said. "I'm inviting you for the festival of my chamber orchestra there. I'm counting on you."

Heavy suitcases bump past on the conveyor belt. Orchestra members kiss one another, thump shoulders, wave with broad arm gestures. They stack their carts high with luggage, instruments and plastic bags filled with chocolate and liquor. Then they go past customs, through the glass doors and embrace their wives, children, husbands. The concertmaster kisses the violist behind a pillar. Minutes later Wanda sees each of them in a separate embrace with their partners in ordinary life.

One by one the people in wrinkled clothes, their heads filled with new memories flashing around and a cloud of airplane air around them, are swallowed by those waiting: women with angry, tense faces, impatient men and a quiet child.

Wanda lifts her suitcase from the belt. Slowly she walks to the exit to find a taxi.

Because of the time difference she can't sleep. In the narrow bed she turns over and over. Stretched, curled-up, with or without pillow. She gets up and goes downstairs. She sits at the kitchen table and looks outside where it slowly turns grey. Someone comes down the stairs. Emma.

"Your door was open. You weren't in bed. How are you? You look awfully pale!"

"It's so strange. It's almost day again. What should I do?"

"If you love him, you have to go back," says Emma. She looks at her folded hands, clenched together on the table. "A man you're crazy about and he about you, you should never let him go." Emma sighs and is silent. Wanda says nothing.

"You're probably still confused because you lost your baby," Emma tries again. "But you still have to talk with him, no matter what. You can stay here for a while until you're back to your old self, but after that you have to do something."

Till I'm back to my old self, thinks Wanda. She has never been herself. Yes, when she plays, then yes. What is being yourself?

She rubs her face. Everything has been cut off: the belly, life with Bouw, the image of herself as a woman in a house. Still, it doesn't feel like a loss. Rather like a necessary clean-up. If only it were morning, then she could play. In four weeks she's leaving for Germany with the Beethoven variations. Her fingers itch.

Time begins to fly, it's the start of whirlwind years of events, faces and places in which Wanda is drifting. The passage of years is marked by music: the recital with all the Debussy preludes, the Schönberg programme, the tour with Brahms' second piano concerto.

Black dresses become worn or are lost and are replaced. The old sound technician dies in the recording studio, and the next time a young woman is sitting ready. Doctor Van Beek looks at her insides for the last time, declares everything in order and retires from practice. The house where she lived with Bouw is sold and unrecognisably rebuilt. Joyce has one child after another and stops playing the violin: once a year they go hiking together for a week with backpacks and rainwear.

After a number of faltering and painful conversations when Wanda can't express herself in words and Bouw sits with a back of steel, they decide to end their marriage. Bouw leaves the Reehof and assumes a policy function at the Department of Public Health. Wanda receives a letter from him when he marries Johanna. The birth announcements of his children no longer reach her; she has moved out of his address book. She doesn't get along well with children; she can't keep up her occasional visits to Frank; and when the conservatory invites her to be a main subject instructor, she needs no time to consider her refusal. She gives one or two master classes in the summer months; she lends her name to the course in exchange for a stay in Salzburg or Siena, but she dreads the confrontation with students. A child of twenty plays a Beethoven sonata in a small hall, people are listening attentively and wait for her comments. She'll have to say something, in a few minutes the child will look at her, questioning, shy, curious. It's hot, the doors stand open and in the cloister outside, harsh light falls around pillars. Wanda sweats.

Every year in December she receives a card from Samuel Silberman. She has her recordings sent to him but has always found an excuse not to go on tour in Israel. From time to time she gives solo performances with his orchestra. It's always a pleasant surprise when, after a rehearsal, he places his hand on her hair for a moment.

She falls in love during tours, for a day, a week, and always with the most taciturn musicians. Afterwards, being alone is a consolation, a relief. Lucas has become famous in America. He stands in front of a large symphony orchestra and with Wanda gives a series of concerts that spark with passion. Just as in the past, they continue in the hotel room the erotic discourse that started on the stage. They make love childishly, playfully and with the certainty that they'll go their own way again. Wanda doesn't ask him about his relationships with men; Lucas doesn't make a claim on her lasting attention. Exhausted, they sleep next to each other in the wide bed. When morning comes, Wanda is awake. Sleep is becoming her enemy, an enemy that gains territory every year. It opens the door to dreams that she cannot get used to. It started insidiously, she blamed it on a strange bed, a room that was too warm, too much wine after a performance. The dreams kept coming, at first now and then, then regularly, in the end always. After a few hours of unconsciousness, Wanda falls on the ice and careless skaters cut off her fingers. Someone forces her to pick up a hammer and to smash her other hand herself. She has to loosen the long, thick bass strings from her grand piano and watch how pale people are strung up with them. Panting and sweating she sits bolt upright, she turns on the light, drinks water and doesn't dare to lie down anymore. She makes a habit of getting up in the middle of the night. She sits in a chair and reads Bach.

"Don't torture yourself like that," says Lucas. "There are remedies for it. Just go to a doctor and let him prescribe something!"

Wanda has black circles under her eyes and trembles with fatigue. She takes the sleeping pills and falls into a dreamless coma. Upon awakening she has lost all sense of passing time. She breathes more freely. But when she sits down at the piano for her morning exercises, she notices that her fingers don't obey. They have become clumsy and don't take one another into consideration. They disregard the practised and agreed-upon cooperation and are deaf to the commands that Wanda sends them. Her body feels like a stiff coat. She has to choose between untroubled sleep and controlled movement. She puts away the pills and reconciles herself to a life of nightly reading of scores. The hours of sleep are wedged between two familiar fears: the fear that frightens her awake from a nightmare and the fear of the sleep which causes her to be wide awake up to three times every night until she finally dozes off.

She travels, she practises, she plays. She turns forty. She is to celebrate her birthday with Joyce who lives south of London with her journalist and her now grown children. Before the stay, Wanda makes a tour of England with a Chopin programme. After the last concert she finds in her hotel a telegram from Guido: "Emma seriously ill. Please call."

Chapter twenty-five

Today it will happen, thought Bouw when he woke up. He didn't know what. Pack up his stuff and drive to Barcelona, maybe. For a start he began throwing everything out of his suitcase and then subjected the valise to a reorganization. Books and papers on the bottom. Shoes as well. Folds shirts again. Order.

He went to drink a cup of coffee in the hotel lobby and looked down over the city. The hotel owner was playing with his son and spoke to Bouw.

"A wonderful morning, are you going for a walk? At the back of the hotel you can go up the mountain. You can't miss the path that leads you over the ridge. Beautiful view. Very wild. You come in the other valley and from there it's easy to walk back."

Why not, thought Bouw. I'm here anyway. While walking you can think well.

He realized that he was in the mood for it once he started the climb. He walked through a tunnel of foliage, a green grotto with damp grass at the bottom. The sun didn't come here. As he climbed, he was more in touch with his body. His calf muscles flexed. His lungs heaved.

The trail followed the mountain ridge and became less steep. The nearby trees were not so tall up here and let the sun through in splotches. The trail had become a wide grass path between mountain meadows, bordered by mossy stone walls. Here and there Bouw saw a neglected house. He let himself be guided by the road itself. Through his head went thoughts that he didn't control. How he had walked with his father in the dunes behind Wassenaar, scurrying in his sandals or tall boots to keep up with the large strides. The mushroom hunt started in the grass at the woods' edge. In the spring his father pointed out the small morels with their cleaved hoods; in the summer the chanterelles appeared, and the fall brought cèpes and Scotch bonnets in enormous fairy rings. In the winter he wore black polished shoes and father was buried.

When he once walked in the same woods with Wanda, chanterelles were no longer to be found, even though it was the right time of the year and perfect humid-warm weather. Imagine that he'd just run into her suddenly. He could see himself stand facing a grey-haired woman and heard himself say clumsy things. How are you these days. What are you doing. What have you done all this time. Furtively look at her bent back. Search for a glimpse of the past in her eyes. How dreadful. More than thirty years. How did he get it into his head. He had once paid a working visit to the Reehof when he was an inspector. He hadn't been there for ten years and walked somewhat wistfully through the halls and the wards. The mentally handicapped looked up from their activities and smiled. "Aha the doctor," they said and continued eating or doing puzzles. Bouw felt surprised. Why weren't they happy to see him after all these years? They acted as if he had still been there yesterday, as if he had stayed with them all these years.

Slightly annoyed he had quickened his pace. At the exit of the pavilion Guus the kitchen helper was waiting for the food cart.

"Doctor! You must have been on vacation? Not me, I work!"

Time doesn't exist, Bouw suddenly realized. Ten years are a week here. It makes no difference. If you were ever there, you'll always stay. He laughed and shook Guus' hand.

In the wall next to the path a seat had been cut and from there you could look into the next valley. Bouw sat down and placed his swollen hands on the cool stone.

At the point where the path started bending down stood a house with walls of stacked slate-grey stone, dark woodwork and small windows. A long, narrow garden ran parallel to the road. A man sat in a wicker chair under a tree. He was around sixty with a calm tanned face and dressed in corduroy trousers and a coarse blue shirt. On the table next to him lay an open book. There also was a cup of coffee. The man was reading a newspaper. He lifted his head and looked out over the valley.

Bouw stood still on the grass path. He smelled a whiff of coffee. He heard the newspaper rustle, he heard the man hum softly, farther away he heard the tinkling of sheep's bells.

No more briefcases, thought Bouw. No annual reports, no meetings. No strategy, no plan. No wife with silk blouses and a pocket-calendar as thick as the bible. No embarrassment about flabbiness. No longer the permanent pressure in his head, the voice that calls out: keep up, lose weight, forward!

Suppose that he comes to her and stays. She has sold her piano, she makes soup in an orange pan. With mushrooms that she has picked in the forest. They each sit at a side of a rough wooden table. In a garden. Suppose that it is peace. Suppose that time freezes. Suppose that he comes home and wants to stay there.

The man in the wicker chair turned his head and saw him standing. He smiled, raised his hand in greeting and then continued reading the paper.

235

Chapter twenty-six

Wanda refuses the plastic tray with food that the stewardess hands her.

Through the weather-beaten window she looks at the sea on which ships as small as her pinkie move slowly and make white stripes that dissolve back into the grey.

She sits with her hands crossed over her shoulders, her head bowed, and her knees crossed. The pilot has started the descent. It would be nice to sleep, but that won't work. She'll let herself be driven to her apartment right away, leave her luggage in the hall and immediately leave again. Guido is waiting for her.

He's making waffles in the familiar kitchen. He presses Wanda against his apron, has her sit down at the table and starts relating what happened. High above the bulging stomach his friendly face hovers in the cooking smoke. The thick, greying hair is too long. He walks in plaid slippers.

"We went to the movies," says Guido, "and then supper. Oysters. It's from the oysters, says the doctor. But I'm fine! There must have been one bad oyster, and Emma ate it. She's so crazy about them. Oysters from Ierseke."

Helplessly he looks at Wanda and shrugs his shoulders. He puts a plate with waffles in front of her.

"Some preserves? Home made. Coffee? I'm happy you've come back. I don't recognize my Emma. She's becoming so impetuous. She says anything that comes into her head. It's not easy to visit her."

When he drives to the hospital, he's still talking. About the kitchen, singing, treacherous oysters. Wanda sees his old hands lying on the steering wheel. Bony joints, brown spots on the skin. She blinks her eyes forcefully to dispel her fatigue. Not back home with him afterwards. She can't manage that. Frightened old man. Can't reassure him. The same hospital. Who says that Mum wants her at her bedside? He, Guido, says so. Because he's frightened. She wants to go away again as quickly as possible.

Two white aprons hang on the inside of the door. Guido and Wanda have to tie them on. They are fumbling in the small scrub room. There is a wash basin where they will have to scrub their hands later, after the visit. In the mirror Wanda sees her own face: tired, tense, old. Guido opens the second door and steps into the room. He clasps a big bouquet like a banner and holds it out.

"Put that away, it stinks," says Emma. She lies half upright in bed. It's dark in the room: gloomy northern light and no lights on. Guido presses a switch, and now a light shines on Emma from halfway behind her head. She looks as if she's just returned from skiing, her skin is orange-brown. Her face and her neck have become thin. Her eyes flash back and forth. Wanda takes the flowers from Guido and puts them in the wash basin behind the door. When she comes back in, Emma is crying.

"I feel so awful, so nauseous. I want out of here, I'm alone all day long. They let me lie in my shit, those stupid bitches!"

"But now we've come," says Guido, "look at this, Wanda is here!"

Emma retches in the small basin that stands on the bedside table. Wanda doesn't want to look at it. She leans with her back against the wall and stares out of the window.

"Wanda! Darling!" Emma's voice sounds happy. She hits the bed with her orange fist. "How nice that you're here! Come and sit by me."

Wanda pulls a stool from under the bed.

"I'm doing so well that I'll surely be able to go home soon. To my sweet Guido. And now you're here too. Did you play? You have to tell me everything!"

Wanda doesn't know what to say. She wants to stroke the strangely coloured hand. Suddenly Emma bursts out.

"Just go. What good are you two? Call the nurse. Bastards, assholes, go away!"

"But sweetheart," says Guido. Emma cries in his arms. Wanda has stood up.

"I'm coming tomorrow during the day," she says. "And Guido in the evening. Is that all right or is it too much?"

"Oh dear, how wonderful. That's lovely. I'm looking forward to it," says Emma with tears in her eyes.

"The doctor says that it's part of it," says Guido in the car. "Lack of inhibition he calls it. She's just confused. I'll take you home, you must be tired."

"She's very sick," says Wanda. "How will it turn out, did the doctor say anything about that?"

Guido shrugs his shoulders. "Wait and see, he said. The liver is infected. She's no longer allowed to drink wine. I'm sure that it will turn out all right."

The next day Emma is bright orange. The whites of her eyes have turned saffron yellow. Limply she lies between the sheets, in a sort of half sleep from which it's difficult to wake her. For half an hour Wanda sits next to the bed, walks down the hall to look for a doctor or nurse and puts on her coat to leave again.

"Hey you! What are you doing?" says Emma with a grating voice.

"It's me, Mum."

Suddenly her mother smiles. "Wanda, of course. It's

better you leave now, dear, I'm feeling sick today. I keep having such pain. I want to sleep. It's impossible here. A hell. You have to take me away; I don't want it any longer! I don't even get normal food here! Look at this goddam mess on my plate!"

Emma has pulled herself up partway, her eyes flame and she spits while she's talking. Wanda feels her hot forehead, she pushes Emma back into the pillows and tucks the blanket in tightly. Emma closes her eyes.

"Your mother has acute liver atrophy," says the doctor. "We're keeping an eye on everything but therapeutically we can't do much, alas."

It's going all wrong, thinks Wanda. She'll burn up like an orange sun. I'll sit here to the last and ask nothing. Until she dies, and I still won't know anything about her. But what do I want to know?

Agitation gnaws at her stomach. Wanda eats poorly and at night she sleeps even less than usual. Every day she goes to the hospital. In her mother's room hangs a strange smell. Acetone? Ammonia? No, a farm smell, thinks Wanda, an attic smell. Like in Stina's attic. Mouse piss.

She sits looking at the body and thinks: soon I won't have a mother anymore, No father. No husband. No child. No brother, or barely. She has no one except for this orange ghost who lies there, dying. She shakes them all off. Or they her. She sees that Emma's eyes have opened and whispers: "Mum?"

Emma looks at her. Does she even recognize me? Does

she still know who she is? Can she still remember her life?

"Wanda, who takes care of Frank?" Emma's voice sounds sluggish and slurred.

"Frank is in the Reehof. They take good care of him there. And Aunt Ida visits him every month."

"Oh yes," says Emma. She sighs. Wanda doesn't dare to breathe deeply, that's how foul the hospital air seems to her. On the bedside table stands a shiny metal basin.

"Egbert was so crazy about Frank," Emma continues whispering. "I couldn't stand it. My own child."

"Papa couldn't stand me," Wanda heard herself speak. She has straightened her back and looks intensely at her mother.

"Where did you get that idea," says Emma. "What nonsense. He just was a difficult man." She has to cough, she pants for breath and holds a handkerchief in front of her mouth.

"It's not nonsense. He never wanted me to be there."

"Go away. I'm sick. Give me that basin. I have to throw up! You're just saying something."

"No!" Wanda screams. "When he was dying he didn't even want to see me! His own daughter!"

Suddenly Emma's bright yellow eyes open wide. She looks at Wanda intently, her mouth open.

"His daughter! Ha!"

The basin slides from her hands and crashes to the floor. Steel on stone. The kitchen. Egbert kneeling on the floor, a kitchen towel in his hands. Emma sobbing with her arms on the table, holding Wanda's gaze with her eyes, so intensely that Wanda froze. The sound of steel on stone.

The door opens. A nurse rushes in and starts pulling Emma up.

"What do you mean?" gasps Wanda.

"You have to stop," says the nurse, "now leave her in peace!"

Wanda takes her mother's face between both of her hands and forces her to listen.

"What do you want to say to me? Say it. Now!"

Emma's eyes turn away. Only yellow can be seen. Her head becomes heavy in Wanda's grasp. Her body slides down.

"It's really better you leave, ma'am," says the nurse. With tears in her eyes, Wanda stands up.

Emma starts vomiting unrestrainedly in the nurse's arms.

With large, springy steps Wanda walks through the halls of the hospital. She kicks against the revolving door. She wants out, to the light and the wind. Once outside she starts running. Breathe deeply. Place one leg after another. Fast. It rains gently but she doesn't notice. Her heart races wildly. It's not until stitches in her side force her to slow down that she notices that she's wet with sweat. Asked the right question. Got the only answer.

Soaking wet she comes home. Surprised, she looks at the small practice piano which stands so bravely amidst stacks

of music. The keyboard irritates her with its stupid regu-
larity. She bangs down the lid. Bong. In her raincoat she
sits down on the sofa. Turns on the light. Dark clouds hang
in front of the window. The trees shine. With folded arms
she pushes against her stomach. Kicks off her shoes. Shivers.
Stares ahead. In here nothing moves. If she sits still, she
sees images from the past: Egbert on the floor next to
Frankie, patiently rolling the ball back and forth, always
slowing it down carefully before it touches the frightened
child. She herself holding Emma's hand, excitedly skipping
along the street, on the way to her first real piano lesson.
Mr De Leon's room with the two grand pianos. The inner
courtyard with the wooden door behind which sound
marching footsteps.

That night Wanda doesn't sleep at all. She sits straight up
on the sofa or paces up and down the room in her clammy
raincoat. Her lips move. She mumbles words. Father, father,
she tries, I have a father. The happy feeling fades and is
lost under numerous questions. Why did Emma never tell
anything, not when Egbert died, not when the war started,
not when Frankie was born? Why didn't she leave Egbert;
if you fall in love with someone else can't you get divorced?
Or did she already love Max before she was married? Did
Oma and Opa say: that piano player, that Jewish guy, you
shouldn't associate with him? Did Emma let herself be
forced into a marriage with a proper lawyer? Did Egbert
know about it?

They made love during the rehearsals, Emma became

pregnant, she was fathered next to the grand piano. Or not? Would she have had a better life then? Different?

Stamping her feet she walks through the room. She wants to know it all, she won't leave before she knows everything.

A suitcase with music is what she received, fingerings are what he left her.

For years on end she was with him every week! He put his hand on her head and spoke only about Bach.

Or was she deceiving herself now?

Outside it becomes light. Wanda finally takes off her coat and makes coffee for herself. The muscles in her legs ache from running. In her head she has a list of questions to take to her mother's sickbed. She wants to fight for the answers. She is going to ask Emma for an accounting, she wants to take a retroactive view of her life and for this she demands help from the woman who has betrayed her through silence.

Like a halo the bright yellow hairs lie spread out against the pillow. In the back of the emaciated hand an IV needle has been stuck to which the nurse attaches a tube which she then checks for the liquid passing through. Wanda freezes on the threshold. The nurse, her hands still busy hanging the bag of fluid, abruptly turns her head to the door and starts.

"Your mother fell into a coma last night. I was just going to call you."

Emma's eyes are closed, the lashes lie like pale moss on her cheeks. Wanda nods and says that it's all right, that it doesn't matter, that she'll warn Guido. She is overcome by a paralysing fatigue and slowly lets herself sink down in a chair against the wall. The waiting begins.

After three days Emma dies without coming out of her ochre-yellow swoon.

Chapter twenty-seven

Wanda stood by the countertop and looked out over the graveyard. She had let the dishpan run full of warm water and moved hands and wrists slowly through the suds. The sharp light of the setting sun brushed over the gravestones and emphatically illuminated the names of the dead .

Dinner. A plate with lettuce, cheese, tomatoes. She dried her hands and took what she felt like from the refrigerator. With the plate in her hand and a piece of bread under her arm she walked to the balcony. She turned her chair so that she had a broad view of the full length of the valley and the vast mountain range behind it. She put her legs on a stool and leaned back with a glass in her hand. Between the low, dark grey clouds that covered the sky and the ridged mountain rim, the sun had free play. Wanda felt the last warmth of the day and peered at the enormous orange disk which was starting to set in the farthest corner of the valley. The light flared out with red, with purple tints. The upper part of the mountain bathed in clarity; in the valley it was already dark and the outlines of trees and farms became shrouded. Now that the sun was setting, you saw that the mountain chain was not the end of the world, but, because of the light, you suspected another land behind it. Distinct lines. Clarity.

Wanda sighed. She didn't care much for clarity. Clarity was terribly overrated. The pianist rendered the theme with transparent clarity, you'd read in the reviews. But what was the point if the theme didn't contrast against a dark base? Clarity was cheap, easy and misleading. It veiled the mysterious obscurity in which the essence of all music was hidden. Did you even know what you heard? That's how it should sound when you played. That's how it was. Schubert clear? Brahms? The clarity maniacs had you believe in a false simplicity. Just listen, the things that appear are so logical and clear. Nothing is enigmatic, everything can be followed easily from beginning to end. A lie. As if you didn't have to search, as if you didn't have to enter a composition blindly, ready to stray in any direction, not too lazy to find a meaning in the most unexpected places. After all, an interpretation wasn't a judgment that was fixed forever. Didn't it happen that an edifice of interpretation that you had built satisfactorily over the years suddenly started to falter and came tumbling down? Behind the

Goldberg Variations lay Goldberg Variations, and behind them still others!

And wasn't clarity bowing down to the listener? Playing for the listener is too dangerous, thought Wanda. You think you're going to conjure up something for him, you want to influence, manipulate, catch and bind him. Nothing but overstatement and arrogance. It's complicated enough to be in conversation with the composer, to come to an understanding with the keys and the mechanism of your instrument. The listener doesn't matter. You may disregard him.

She ate bread with cheese and pricked into the salad with her fork. The sun disappeared unexpectedly fast behind the mountains.

248

Wanda stood up and wiped her hands on her skirt. She turned around and saw the grand piano in the dark room waiting for her with its wide open jaw. She went inside and turned on the lamp. She left the doors open, soon the coolness of the evening would come. How helpless and silent it stood there, the beast. It was time that they came to an understanding. All fighters had been struck down or had disappeared, only this small area of the battlefield was left. She stepped up to the instrument.

"And now it's between the two of us, Bösendorfer!"

Chapter twenty-eight

T he road to the hall of the crematorium is filled with
carelessly parked cars. On the path lie loose pebbles which
shoot up under Wanda's footsteps and end up in her shoes. At
the entrance she bends down to empty them out. Corpulent
people in stiff hairdos and colourful shawls over black clothes
walk past her. Snatches of perfume. Singers.

Aunt Ida has become thin. Her daughter Suze is there
too, she shakes Wanda's hand shyly and points to her four
grown children. Suze herself is tall also; she has a fleshy
face with grey curly hair around it. They all sit down in
the first row; Guido, distressed with grief, between Wanda
and Ida.

In that coffin, thinks Wanda. There she lies, greyish
yellow from all her secrets. Soon she'll be cremated. Soon

she'll sink down, with the bouquet of red roses from Guido on top of the lid.

Wanda pushes her heels firmly against the floor and holds her fists tightly clenched. She stares through the wide window behind the coffin. A park with urns and stones. In the distance a man wearing a cap is pushing a wheelbarrow.

The background music is idiotic. A Bach aria with a stupid sentimental text, *Ich habe genug* or *Es ist vollbracht*, accompanied by a Hammond organ. Very softly, the words can barely be understood. They should be playing the *Fledermaus*: *Glücklich ist . . . wer vergist . . . was doch nicht zu ändern ist*. That's Emma's favourite song, that music should be blaring through the hall.

Speeches. A gentleman from the light opera company. A pupil with a pleasant, deep voice. They say nice things. Then Aunt Ida steps forward. The tattered raincoat hangs sloppily around her tall, straight body. Aunt Ida speaks the truth, she talks about the war, about the birth of a handicapped child and about Egbert's death. "Wanda with her musical gifts has always been a great consolation to my sister," she says.

Wanda is startled. The truth, but not the complete truth. She squeezes her hands into bullets. Ida continues speaking about the last years of Emma's life, how happy she was with Guido, how wonderful it was to resume her singing career. Tears trickle down Guido's cheeks when he briefly thanks those present for their concern. The inane music starts up once again. The coffin is lowered.

"You have to consider that it was a totally different time," says Aunt Ida. "It was normal that daughters did what their parents said."

Wanda listens. She has a sore throat. In the hall it felt as if her throat had been screwed shut. Now that she is walking through the urn park with her aunt, she feels with every question she poses that it's raw and red inside.

"Max De Leon. The very name! Father and mother thought it was a dangerous development. He encouraged her to go on the stage. They'd rather not have had that, you know. And Emma was so terribly in love with him. At home there were quarrels about it. Agreements that she would no longer see him. Which of course she did anyway, and then there followed another scene. They even considered sending Emma to Vienna, to study. That didn't go through, I think for political reasons. Then he disappeared, for a long time, certainly more than a year as I remember. Perhaps he had to work abroad, I don't know. But during that time Egbert came forward. He'd been crazy about Emma for years and took the opportunity. His parents were friends of father and mother."

Ida is flushed from the talking. The sentences flow without any encouragement, she wants to get it off her chest, it has to come out. Arm in arm the two women keep walking the same circle.

"Then there was a wedding. If Emma had really not wanted it, it wouldn't have happened. I do think that she opted for certainty. She didn't talk about it. Then Max returned. I was already living in Montfoort, we didn't see each other often. I did think that she had an affair with him, but she never really told me. She didn't know how to handle it. She didn't want to hurt Egbert. You were born. No one said anything, that was the simplest. That's how it was then."

Suddenly Wanda is terribly fed up with the conversation. Her shoulders, back and legs hurt. She wants to go home and crawl under as many blankets as possible.

After a few days Wanda calls Guido who is staying with his sister in Antwerp to recover. She asks him for permission to look through Emma's papers. Despite his sorrow, his voice sounds friendly and concerned. She has to keep eating properly, he says, and at night have a cognac to get to sleep. And not worry!

Wanda turns the whole house inside out and afterwards puts everything back neatly. The small desk in the music room, the music cabinet, the linen closet, the drawers with underwear, the suitcases and boxes in the attic – everything is examined and nothing is found. Max as well as Egbert have been erased from Emma's life.

The next day Wanda's muscles ache throughout her body. On the piano lie the thick music books with the Brahms variations that she will record in Germany next month. She opens the lid, wants to sit down but notices that she doesn't feel like it. Her hands hurt when she thinks of playing the piano. It's because of all the lugging of Emma's stuff, she thinks. And she's not yet in the mood for practising. She just has to take a few days rest.

I'll get rid of it by playing, thinks Wanda, when the pain stays. She does the familiar exercises and tries to let herself get swept away by Brahms. There remains an irritated nagging in her thumb joints.

After the recordings she takes a vacation and walks with Joyce through hilly English landscapes. Every morning she lies in a hot bath for half an hour to get rid of the night's stiffness. At the thought of concerts and tours, she is caught unawares by a slight reluctance which she can hardly believe. She continues playing.

Every autumn her complaints worsen. Every summer brings relief. Wanda attributes the fact that playing the piano no longer fulfils and satisfies her as it did formerly to the trouble it costs and the pain which she has to combat. During five difficult years there is one whole February with the joy and suppleness of old times. In Israel, where she tours with old Silberman and his chamber orchestra. Her joints seem to have shrunk, passing the thumb under goes smoothly, and the music comes from under her hands as it was meant to. She feels like a welcome guest in this strange country, and she enjoys the dry air and the bright sun.

When she is back home again, fatigue hits hard. She lies in bed until the middle of the day without sleeping.

She doesn't feel like doing anything. The joints of her wrists and fingers seem to be filled with nasty sharp crystals that prick and smart worse when she plays. She can no longer spread her hands without screaming out in pain.

"Rheumatoid arthritis." The doctor mumbles to himself while he writes something on a prescription. "You need absolute rest. Now."

"That's impossible," says Wanda. "In three weeks I'm going to Italy. And sometimes nothing bothers me, like when I was in Israel. I'm not sick."

The doctor looks at her. He's younger than I, thinks Wanda. He knows what's wrong with me. He's right.

"Rest, analgesics and something to counteract the infection. We'll start with that. I fear that you'll have to cancel your tour. You'll end up in a wheelchair if we don't take action. You have neglected it for years."

Wanda leans back in the chair. Rest. She listens. The doctors talks about stress, fever, humidity and cold, about salubrious and insalubrious climate conditions, about thermal baths and gold injections.

I'm stopping, thinks Wanda. She has played all her life, it's been enough. She'll leave the piano behind, she's going to live on a mountain in the sun. Enough.

With stiff fingers she grips the steering wheel of the car. She should be crying, she thinks, her career lies in ruins, everything has been for naught, the decline has begun. But she feels good. Where in the world will she live? She can choose. She doesn't have to do anything anymore. No more asking, no more begging, no more extorting. From now on she will only *be*.

Chapter twenty-nine

Twilight was setting in when Bouw came back to the hotel. He was thirsty, he was dead tired and his legs felt weak. On the terrace a waiter was busy setting the tables for dinner. Automatically Bouw walked to his room to wash. It wasn't until he was getting dressed in clean clothes that he suddenly realized that he had to get away. He grabbed together his toiletries, stuffed his sweaty walking clothes in a plastic bag and closed his suitcase. When he came storming down the stairs, the hotel owner looked at him surprised.

"Are you leaving already? But what about dinner? You have paid!"

"I'm sorry," said Bouw. "I suddenly have to leave, something has come up, please excuse me. It's an excellent hotel, really."

He pushed open the roof while he was driving. The cool evening air had a calming effect, as did the speed with which he left the town. I'll just drive to the coast, how far would that be? Or I'll sleep somewhere along the highway, not in a fairy-tale village like this. Now to the conference. Read papers, have meetings, call Johanna. No longer walk through streets where sulphur vapour suddenly spirals up along your body. No longer roaming and wretched in pursuit of the past. He held the steering wheel loosely at the bottom. His shoulders relaxed. He hummed a melody. The motor sang.

At the exit to the village, he turned up the mountain road. The manoeuvring in the hairpin turns had left him no time for thinking. Suddenly he stood on a small plaza in front of a dilapidated hotel. Just look for a moment, he thought, just see where she lives, nothing more. He parked next to the hotel and went in. It smelled of soup. A sturdy woman in an apron asked good-naturedly if he wanted to eat. He sat at a table on which lay a red and white checked tablecloth and suddenly felt an immense hunger. The woman gave him wine in a water glass, leek soup and stewed rabbit with green beans. Bouw finished everything.

From behind the bar she asked him how it was. There were no other guests. Bouw leaned back and let the conversation take its course. She always cooked herself, she said, and had for thirty-five years. No, not many people came here. One or two tourists who didn't want to be down below. Or the nature lovers who went hiking in the mountains. People from the village? They didn't eat here, at most sometimes when there was a festival. Young people didn't live here much anymore, he was right about that. They went to work in Toulouse and came back twice a year in a big car with suitcases filled with clothes. The houses were sold, sometimes to foreigners, yes. A woman, a pianist? Oh, *she*, with the gloves. Yes certainly, she knew her well, already for years. It's nearby, the top house, next to the graveyard. She was here just this morning, she comes almost every day. Straight up along the street, you can't help running into it!

In her enthusiasm Françoise practically pushed Bouw out the door. Outside it was pitch black. Hesitating, he followed the path up. In a yellow-lit room he saw a couple sitting in front of a television set. A family sat eating, a man was looking at a newspaper under a floor lamp. No one was on the street.

A small car stood close to the house. Bouw looked inside: a shopping bag, an umbrella on the back seat, indistinct clutter and road maps on the floor. He turned his head away fast. There was no name on the wide wooden front door. There was a mailbox and a bell, but he walked around the corner and found the entrance to the graveyard. Carefully he opened the gate. Light came out of the windows at the back of the house. Bouw looked inside surreptitiously and saw dishes standing, a colander and a red dishwashing basin.

Startled he continued walking and hid behind the

upright gravestones. He fled all the way to the end of the graveyard, to the point where the stone enclosure demarcated the rough plane lying behind it. There he turned around. He saw a balcony with big pots full of blue flowers. Slowly he started walking in the direction of the house. Then faster, with big steps stumbling between the gravestones, bumping his feet against rocks and vases, as if he just wanted to run into the room, calling out that he was there.

An ornamental iron chain slammed against his shins, he cursed, almost fell and panting, sat down on a tombstone.

Chapter thirty

Once a journalist had come, all the way from Amsterdam, to write an article about her. She had agreed because he was nice and was a good listener. Dumbfounded he had observed that she didn't have a piano in her house. Didn't she miss playing terribly?

It wasn't until he had left that Wanda could think about that calmly. Miss? No. Barely. The first years in these mountains had been so filled with furnishing the house, getting acquainted with the surroundings and the regimen imposed by her illness, that she didn't get around to missing. There had been the liberation of finally being able to reflect, read books and write letters. She had grown and cared for the blue flowers on the balcony. When she longed for music, she listened to the radio or read a score. Her whole repertory was stored in her memory so that she could play a piece in her head whenever she wanted. If she didn't know something for sure, she looked it up in the music cabinet. Was that missing? She didn't like to listen to piano pieces, she preferred orchestral works or chamber music, that was true. Was it because of an unbearable desire for piano playing or because of the edifice of memories and associations that was connected to her piano repertoire?

She didn't care. She had bought a Bösendorfer and it stood here, in her own balcony room. Of course she had yearned. Her body had experienced yearnings, the left arm wanted to play a rotating bass extending over chords, with shoulder, elbow and wrist. The right one yearned for a bouncing, rising octave run and wanted to be pushed up high at the end.

The most vehement was her nostalgia for the first chord. Sit down. Feel the back and shoulders. Press the right pedal so that all the open strings lie waiting to be touched by the hammers or to vibrate along. The hands hovered above the keyboard, they already carried the chord within them; the fingers were aware of position and weight, they yearned ardently for ivory and ebony; the fingertips craved the keys. Descending. The rising sound. The door to music has been pushed open.

The lit square of the window looks like a painting of a sitting woman. She plays: a legato bass line with a meandering melody above it. The sound fans out into the evening, is distorted above the roofs of the houses and lost in the valley. The man sitting on the stone listens. Between his legs his hands hang down like two tired, white animals. He has turned his head to the window, it seems as if he wants to smell and taste the sounds. Hungrily he sucks the music up inside him. He knows it, Bach, what is it, the Italian Concerto or something, beautiful. He sees how the woman bends her body along with the low tones, how sometimes she tilts her head for a moment to hear the melody better which she then breaks off suddenly.

A silvery light falls over graveyard and balcony. Mute and brilliant the moon hangs above the jagged mountains and the dark valley.

About the author

Anna Enquist
Photo by Vincent Mentzel

Anna Enquist a psychoanalyst and classically trained musician, was born in 1945. A few years ago she began to write poetry, as she said, 'from one day to the next'. Today, she is one of the Netherlands' most popular poets and novelists, with a large readership in Germany, Switzerland, Austria and Sweden.

The Secret is her second novel, and won the 1997 Dutch Readers Prize as Book of the Year. It has been a remarkable best seller, with over 250,000 copies sold in the Netherlands.

The fonts used in this book are from the Garamond and Akzidenz Grotesk families.